"Save you— I've been—

Mac towered a— — emanating from every inch of him. "What a fun summer, to have a fling with a yokel, then hightail it back to Los Angeles when things start turning serious here. Well, 'serious' is off. You've had your fun and I've had mine. We're even now, and quits!"

"No, Mac, please listen." Amanda was scared. Had she ruined everything by her desire for secrecy, by her wish to be just plain Mandy Smith for a summer?

"Next time," Mac went on, "pretend a little more, Amanda. At least tell a guy once that you love him, even though it would be a lie, too."

"I do. It's not a lie, Mac!"

Barbara McMahon and her two daughters share their home in the San Francisco Bay area with one dog, two cats and a pair of rabbits. Before settling down to work for a computer software company, her stint as an airline stewardess took her all over the world. But her favorite place remains the Sierra Nevada mountains where one day she hopes to live and write full-time.

Books by Barbara McMahon

HARLEQUIN ROMANCE
2643—COME INTO THE SUN

These books may be available at your local bookseller.

Don't miss any of our special offers. Write to us at the following address for information on our newest releases.

Harlequin Reader Service
901 Fuhrmann Blvd., P.O. Box 1397, Buffalo, NY   14240
Canadian address: P.O. Box 2800, Postal Station A,
5170 Yonge St., Willowdale, Ont.   M2N 6J3

Bluebells on the Hill

Barbara McMahon

Harlequin Books

TORONTO • NEW YORK • LONDON
AMSTERDAM • PARIS • SYDNEY • HAMBURG
STOCKHOLM • ATHENS • TOKYO • MILAN

Original hardcover edition published in 1986
by Mills & Boon Limited

ISBN 0-373-02777-X

Harlequin Romance first edition July 1986

CHAPTER ONE

AMANDA SMITH alighted from the bus, shocked as the heat of the day engulfed her. She had been travelling in comfort for hours, even verging on being too cool, as the bus had sped its way eastward from the coast. Aware of the brightness of the cloudless day through the tinted windows, but not the heat. The hot noonday sun shone down with searing rays, the lack of breeze ensuring that the heat hung close to the earth.

Looking around, she smiled. Twice before she had passed through Timber, California. Now she was here for a long visit, to look into the possibilities of settling here on a semi-permanent basis. As much as her job would permit.

The small main street shimmered beneath the relentless sun, heat waves distorting the shop fronts and reflecting non-existent puddles on the asphalt road. Slowly she walked along the side of the bus, awaiting the driver who would unload her cases. Unload hers alone, it appeared, as no one else had disembarked. Unload and drive on.

The depot for Timber consisted of a small wooden attachment to the gas station: one window for tickets, a wooden bench serving as the waiting area. What did a person do in the rain? she wondered idly as she waited for her luggage.

'I'll have your things in a jiffy, miss.' The bus driver joined her on the hot pavement. With a quick jerk, he opened the side panel, revealing the capacious luggage compartment. Reaching among the bags, he unerringly pulled out her large, plaid, soft-sided suitcase, and the battered guitar case.

'These all, right, miss?'

'Yes, thanks.' Amanda smiled at him.

Slamming down the compartment door, he sketched a small salute and returned to the bus. Amanda gathered up her pieces, and approached the ticket window. She had passed through this small mountain town before, across the narrow bridge on the approach to Timber—a concrete structure spanning the Mokelumne River, connecting Timber with the western part of the state. This time, though, she was not passing through. She was stopping for a while. Staying for a while.

Her dark hair absorbing the heat, Amanda felt the full strength of the sun beating through to her scalp. Perspiration beaded on her forehead, ran between her breasts. She took a deep breath. It didn't help; the air was hot, still.

Dropping her bags near the building, she turned to watch the bus as it lumbered down the street and began its climb as the highway wound upwards, heading north, to greater heights.

For a town named Timber, the most notable aspect of the trees was the lack of them. True, at the city limits, the Sierra forest began, but within sight of her eyes there were few trees, none of great size or age. Her eyes followed the bus until it rounded the bend and was lost from view. She dropped her gaze closer.

The town was small. This she had known, but the actual sight of it from the ground only emphasised it. From the furthermost building to the bus depot was not two city blocks in length, if that. She could see the entire town from her vantage point.

Of course, that was what she was seeking. A small community, as different from the cities she had been working in as she could find. This place was perfect. Few cars, no garish neon signs, and only a couple of buildings taller than a single storey. Smiling again,

Amanda felt a warm welcoming flow through her, a strong feeling of nostalgia, of *déjà vu*, and of homecoming.

The fronts to the various stores and shops were irregular and without pattern. Two were two-storeyed, others low, still others with a high façade masking their small status. Red was a popular colour; she counted five stores painted red. White was predominant, with beige, blue and yellow also in evidence. There was even a brick building to her left, an unusual sight in the Sierra Nevada.

'Can I help you?'

She turned to find a small, wizened man at the ticket window gravely watching her.

'Is there somewhere I can leave my luggage for a while?' she asked, indicating the pieces lying by her feet.

'Sure, put them on the bench. I'll keep an eye on them for you. They'll be OK there.'

Frowning with hesitation, she looked at the bench, out of direct view from his window. Then she glanced down the sleepy street. The few people in sight on the pavements chatted easily with one another, calling out friendly greetings, nodding as they passed. No one was interested in her or her luggage.

She turned back. 'Thank you, I won't be too long.' Pushing the heavy suitcase against the building, she rested the guitar case against it. With a smile, she turned back to the ticket agent.

'I'll watch 'em, miss, don't you fret.' He looked like somebody's grandfather.

She nodded, hitching her shoulder bag up higher. Again she surveyed the town, this time seeking a specific place, slowly moving to an establishment which caught her eye.

'Gold Country Properties', the sign hanging before the large window proclaimed. It was faded, weathered, hanging from rusty hinges, stationary in the hot sun. A dozen or so photos were taped to the window, each a picture of a house, or an expanse of land, presumably for sale.

She pushed on the glass door; it opened inward. There were only two people in the office: a grey-haired man seated behind a desk in the rear of the large room, and an equally grey woman seated opposite him. While there were three other desks in the office, with evidence of occupation, phones, maps, survey books, their owners were absent. Perhaps showing property.

Amanda wasn't sure the couple in the rear had heard her and she waited patiently for them to finish. The older woman was speaking; she had a loud, whiny voice.

'. . . but not to Mac. I'm absolutely adamant about that, Martin. Not to Mac!'

'Be reasonable, Cora.' The man was patient, as one who had been over this before. 'No one else will take it. If you are leaving, why do you care who gets it? Take what money you can get and go on along to Phoenix. Julie'll be so glad to have you close. Forget us here.'

'No, Martin, not to Mac.' She was firm. 'How do you know no one else will take it? Advertise and find out.'

'Cora, if I advertise, I have to sell it to whoever offers the best price. It's the law. I cannot refuse to accept an offer just because it comes from someone you don't like.'

'Then don't advertise,' she muttered.

'Then nobody will know it is available and you'll never get it sold.' He leaned back in his chair. 'It's not worth much anyway. It's old, away from town, no near neighbours, few amenities, surrounded by trees and precious little else. You'll be hard pressed to find anyone who wants a place like that Cora, be realistic.'

'I might be interested,' Amanda spoke up.

The woman swivelled round to see who had spoken. The man leaned sideways in his chair to see around Cora. They saw the young woman by the door. She was tall, thin. Skinny, almost, the man thought. Her dark hair was drawn back in a single plait down her back. Large tinted glasses hid her expression like a mask.

'Who are you?' the woman named Cora asked.

'My name is Mandy Smith.' The young woman walked back.

'Not from around here, are you, miss?' the man asked, his tone more cordial than Cora's. She could be, her faded jeans, scuffed boots and cotton shirt the same attire everyone wore nowadays. Everybody young, that was.

'No, but I'm interested in settling here. I came in to find a place.'

He looked at her for a moment, rubbing his chin, obviously phrasing his words carefully. 'The, uh, place in question is for sale, not for rent.'

'Yes, so I gathered from your conversation. I would like to see it. I might be interested in it.'

'It's out of town a few miles,' he said.

'With no near neighbours and lots of trees,' she repeated.

'Yes, that's right, girl,' the old woman said. 'It's a mite run down, needs a little work, but it's real pleasant to sit out on the porch and hear the breeze rustle through the trees.' She turned back to the man. 'Take her up, Martin. Let her see what it's like.'

'There's nobody here, Cora, to answer the phone. I can't just leave.'

'I'll answer them, if they ring. Just till Dottie comes back. Go on, Martin. Miss Smith might want it.'

'It's for sale,' Martin said again, as if explaining an important fact to a child.

'Don't let my clothes mislead you,' Amanda said gently. 'If I like it, I can afford it.'

'Go on, Martin,' Cora urged.

'OK, OK.' He rose, picked up his hat from the nearby rack and came around his desk. 'OK, young lady, we'll go see it. Mind the phone, Cora.'

Amanda preceded him from the office, pausing on the pavement. 'I don't have a car.'

'No problem, we'll go in mine. This way.' Martin led the way up the street a few yards. Opening the door of a Chevy Blazer, he motioned her in.

'I'm Martin Roberts, own the place.' He nodded back to the office as he climbed into the Blazer. 'Sales are picking up a little, now that summer's started. My other people are out showing property. Mostly to weekenders,' he tacked on as an afterthought.

He started his vehicle.

Martin Roberts didn't talk as they drove through Timber. No hard sales pitch here, Amanda thought, amused. Not that she wanted one; she was content to gaze out the window, watching for landmarks and enjoying the scenery as they left the man-made buildings behind and sped along the highway that cut through the forest, following the route the bus had taken only a short time before.

Immediately the air felt cooler, the difference between the hot town and the cooler highway due to the lofty trees enclosing the asphalt strip, sheltering it, shading it, as it slashed its way up the mountain.

It was only a few minutes before Martin slowed to turn into a dirt and gravel side-road. Not *so* far out of town.

'This leads to Cora's place. She only has a small cabin and an acre or so of land. All the rest here belongs to Mac. His land completely encircles Cora's.

This road is an easement. No problem getting to and from the highway. Got electricity and city water.'

Amanda listened to his description, his explanations, smiling at the 'city water' phrase. Well, to each his own. If the folks of Timber considered Timber a city, why not? It certainly was not like the cities she was familiar with, but no matter.

Amanda wondered again why Cora was so adamant about refusing to sell to this Mac. It would make sense to sell to him, to enable the land to become part of the property which surrounded it. To have a ready, willing buyer, rather than depend upon chance. Maybe this property wouldn't be for her after all. Maybe Mac would still get it.

'Why won't Cora sell it to Mac?' she asked aloud.

'Old family feud. Cora wants to go to Arizona to be near her daughter. Needs to sell this place, but because of something that happened years ago, she refuses to sell it to Mac. Too bad, it's the logical thing.'

There were tall Ponderosa pines, Douglas firs and California cedars growing on both sides of the road. A mature madrone across the drive sheltered an opening to a pretty, gently sloping, grassy meadow on the left. Ahead, a smaller, rutted track branched off to the right. Martin turned on to it and stopped.

The cabin was old, and tired. A piece was missing from part of the roof, near the left edge. The front was faded and shabby. Its large wooden veranda gave the place its only attractive feature, yet it, too, needed repair.

Amanda stared at it, intrigued. It looked forlorn and forgotten. She thought that Cora lived in it, now, but it was hard to believe. There was a definite air of total desertion about the place. Perhaps Cora had abandoned it, had given up caring, knowing it was only a question of time before she left.

Amanda felt an unaccustomed stirring of anticipation. Maybe she could fix it up. Make it pretty and . . . and happy again. It would be a change from her current life. A new challenge. A pleasant interlude. In that instant she knew she wanted it, would have it if at all possible. Too bad for Mac; this property would be hers!

There were three steps up to the front deck. Amanda followed Martin Roberts into the cabin, eager to see the rest of the place. The living room was a good size, easily half the house. To the left, a large pot-bellied stove, for heat in the colder months. Near the door to the kitchen, Cora had placed a table and chairs for a dining area. The furniture was old and worn, the chair seats faded to nondescript grey. Amanda glanced around, ideas spinning. A few coats of paint, some bright spots of colour here and there, would turn it all around. Very little work, really, if the structure were sound.

'Bedrooms through here.' Martin led the way.

Definitely *not* a hard sell, that's for sure, Amanda thought again. Well, if she bought it, it would certainly be all her own doing.

There were two bedrooms, one smaller one with a single bed. She peeked in. It was fairly clean, though plain. No pictures on the walls, bare floor and dirty windows. The master bedroom was larger, with windows on two walls, but not much more in the way of decorations.

The trees did not grow as densely behind the cabin as in front. Amanda moved to see the view from the back. The land gradually inclined upward, not steeply, opening to a grassy lea. She felt her throat tighten at the beauty before her. The hill was losing its rich spring green colour as the summer took hold, browning the grass. It was still quietly pretty. A short distance from the house, to the right, a bank of bluebells nodded in the afternoon sun. As Amanda's eyes travelled further, she took in the deep green of the rising pines; the wrought, top-heavy cedars contrasting sharply with the pale, brassy blue of the cloudless sky.

'I like this place,' she said softly. She looked around the room and smiled. Returning to the living room, she gazed out of the smudged window at the trees that grew so straight, so tall, with dark bark and two shades of green. What a difference from city concrete. She crossed over to the sofa and sat down, regarding Martin deliberately.

'Does the furniture come with the place?'

He stared down at her in disbelief. 'You are serious? You would consider this place?' He looked around as if trying to see what would appeal to anyone.

'Yes, I'm serious. Is the furniture included?'

He sank down on a nearby chair. 'I don't know. We can ask Cora. Mac won't like it, though, if Cora sells to someone else.' He shook his head.

'I'm sure Mac will survive,' she said drily. 'Cora's evidently been here some time.'

'Yes, but if he knew she was planning to leave, he'd sure try to get this place.' Martin waved his hand. 'All the surrounding land is his. This would fill it in.'

She nodded. 'I know. How much?'

'I don't know.' Martin hesitated. 'Forty-five?'

Narrowing her eyes in consideration, Amanda did not answer right away. Finally, 'OK, *if* Cora leaves the furniture, and the structural inspection is OK.'

He nodded. 'We can see. I can have the inspection done tomorrow.' He took out a handkerchief and mopped his forehead, pushing his hat back to reach his brow. Replacing his hat, he stood. 'Want to see around the property?'

'Of course!' Amanda rose eagerly. How much of the land would be hers?

They tramped around the cabin, Martin remaining quiet during most of the tour, only pointing out boundaries when they reached them. The more Amanda took in the property, the more she wanted it. What was it that gave her such a sense of homecoming? She was not from around here, not even a native Californian, yet she felt as if she belonged; as if the mountains were calling her home.

Neither spoke on the short drive back to town. Martin had a look of growing disapproval on his face. Amanda mentally reviewed her property. There had even been a small stream cutting through one corner of her land. She was already calling it hers. She hoped Cora would be agreeable to the terms. If not, she shrugged, there would be other properties.

Yes, but with bluebells nodding on the hill? With a stream running through it? She shook her head. Cora had to sell!

Cora looked up eagerly from the magazine she was reading when they returned, still the only occupant of the office. 'Well, did you like it? Do you want it?'

Amanda smiled at her. 'I did like it and I would be interested in it. If,' she cautioned, 'it is structurally sound. Also, if you would consider leaving the furniture.'

Cora's face clouded. 'Oh, the furniture. I don't know. I hadn't thought about it.' She fell quiet while Martin went to take his chair. Amanda moved to sit at his desk, in the chair next to Cora.

'Landsakes, nothing there worth much. I will need to take the sofa and one bed, but the table and other bed can stay. If you want them, have them,' Cora decided.

'When can I take possession?' Amanda asked Martin.

'Well, that depends,' Martin said slowly. 'First we have to get the credit approvals, then the bank does the credit check, appraisal . .' He doodled figures on his notepad. 'Probably a month or so, if all goes well.'

'So long?' Cora whined. 'I could go so much sooner.'

'I don't need a credit check,' Amanda said quietly, 'I plan to write a cheque.'

Two pair of eyes stared at her.

'Write a cheque,' Cora repeated.

'I thought the price we discussed was forty-five thousand dollars,' Martin said, jogging her memory.

Cora's eyes widened at the figure mentioned, but she kept quiet.

'Yes, with furniture. I'd like possession as soon as possible, if the inspection is all right. Not,' she was firm, 'in a month.'

Martin was at a loss for words.

'I can write the cheque now, and you can call my bank for verification of funds. I have identification.' She was matter-of-fact, assured, taking her cheque book from her purse. She took a pen from Martin's desk and began to write. Before signing her name, she paused and looked up.

'I do have another condition, in addition to the furniture. I don't want it to get out how I purchased the house.'

Cora shook her head, her expression still one of stunned disbelief. Write a cheque for a house!

'No, we won't say anything,' Martin added.

'I'd like to move in as soon as I can,' Amanda said, signing her name with a flourish. 'Do I make it payable to Cora or the real estate firm?'

'First Title Trust Company. They will handle escrow, though I don't think they have ever had a house paid for all at once before.'

When Amanda had filled in the name she ripped the cheque from her book and handed it across. Martin took the cheque and looked at it. Glancing at his watch, he pulled the phone closer and dialled the number of the bank printed on the face of the cheque.

Amanda sat calmly watching him as he spoke, the tinted glasses hiding her expression.

Cora licked her lips. Her eyes darted from the cheque to Amanda, and back to Martin as he identified himself, asked for verification, and waited for a senior bank official to respond to his questions. While Cora was on edge as the minutes dragged by, Amanda was serene and quiet.

'Hello, Mr Fairfield, this is Martin Roberts. I'm a real estate broker. I have a cheque for a house that a Miss Amanda Smith wishes to purchase. I'm calling to verify the funds are in the account. Your teller forwarded my call to you.' He paused while the official on the other end spoke. 'Sure, she's tall and thin, with black hair. It's long.' He peered at Amanda. 'What colour are your eyes?' he asked politely.

With an amused smile, she removed her tinted glasses, revealing beautiful, clear blue eyes, the dark lashes surrounding them needing no artificial aids to enhance their loveliness.

'Yes, Mr Fairfield, it's her.' He spoke to the phone, but did not take his gaze from Amanda.

Cora looked at her, a puzzled frown on her face.

Martin's eyes widened and he looked confused. 'But ... No, that's fine. We just didn't realise. Yes, of course. Thank you.' Slowly he replaced the receiver.

'Amanda,' he said, still looking at her. '*Amanda*.'

She inclined her head. 'Yes, but I'm travelling, um, incognito as it were for the summer. The last few years have been very hectic. Exciting and fun, you realise, but tiring and a strain. I just want to relax, rest. Maybe write a song or two. Just be myself for a while.' She leaned forward in her chair. 'Please help me find a small place for myself in Timber, Mr Roberts. I will be a good neighbour. Just lend me some support. I want to be just plain Mandy Smith for a while. Not a celebrity, not sought after for what I do, but liked, or disliked, for myself. Just for myself. I want to be an ordinary person again, for a while. For a summer. Can you understand that, Mr Roberts?'

He nodded. 'Martin,' he said, as if still in a daze.

'Would someone please tell me what is going on?' Cora broke in fretfully. 'Is the cheque good?'

'Oh, yes, Cora. Today is your lucky day. This cheque is very good. When you sign over your deed, the place becomes Miss Smith's and you are forty-five thousand dollars ahead.'

Cora sat back. 'I still can't believe anyone can just write a cheque for that amount.'

'Anyone probably cannot. This is Amanda. I know you've heard her songs: *Riverboat Gambler*, *Sing the Mountain Down*.'

Cora's head jerked round. 'Is it true? Of course. I thought you looked a little familiar without the glasses. I've seen your albums. I always thought they had been touched up, but your eyes are real. You're a right pretty gal, Miss Smith.'

Amanda smiled. 'Thank you. My hair's different, too,' she volunteered.

'Yes, I remember it as curly and wavy and sort of falling down.'

'This is my disguise, such as it is. Do we have a deal, Mrs Rosefeld?'

'We do indeed. We do indeed.' Cora turned a beaming face to Martin. 'There, I knew I could sell it to someone other than Mac!' she said triumphantly.

CHAPTER TWO

AMANDA was awake, but still lying in bed, luxuriating in the knowledge that she needn't get up now, or any time this morning, if she didn't want to. She stretched lazily, rolled over on her side and gazed out the back window. From her pillow she could see some of her hill, and a small section of the bluebells, bright and fresh in the early morning sun. Watching them, she felt a warm sense of contentment.

It was hard to believe that, even with all the money she had made over the last years, this was the first piece of property she had owned. Shrewd investments, contributions to charities, money sent home; but not one piece of property until now. She hugged herself with glee, a pleased smile spreading across her face. *Now* she owned land, and a house, albeit a rather small, run-down one. But it held charm and appeal for her. It belonged to her and her alone. She would plan and instigate its resurgence as a desirable abode, use it as a refuge, a haven for her when the pressures of her chosen field got too much. She was beholden to no one. What she chose to do to the property was solely her own decision, and she was excited at the prospect.

Letting her eyes wander around the room, Amanda reflected on how different it was to wake up in this room compared to the rooms she usually woke in. The others had the modern similarity found in all hotels today. This rustic, shabby room was a study in contrast, with its old curtains, bare floor, shabby furniture. It would be a pleasant place, when she refurnished it, painted and decorated it a little. Until then, it would suffice just as it was.

Hard to believe that she had arrived in Timber only two days ago. It was a small, almost forgotten little town in the Sierra Nevada range. Its glorious heyday had been generations before, when gold fever prevailed and men spent their time and lives searching for the precious metal in California's Mother Lode. These strong, rugged mountains still held over twice the gold that had ever been taken from them. She smiled again, dreamily. Maybe she'd strike it rich here. It was there, only waiting to be found. First chance she got, she'd try panning in her creek.

In the meantime, it was pleasant to just lie in bed, no deadlines to meet, no new city to travel to before night. Just peace and quiet and tranquillity. She would recharge, sooth her jangled nerves and try writing again. She had loved writing songs almost more than performing them, but had got away from it lately with the hectic schedule she had been following.

Though, she acknowledged to herself, she also enjoyed the crowds, the applause for a job well done, a favourite song sung for an enthusiastic audience. She would have it again, but not just yet. This summer, at least, would be just for her.

The sun was well up in the sky before Amanda arose. Cora Rosefeld had left her well situated, leaving a set of linen and a few cooking utensils in addition to the furniture she had included in the deal. Cora had even seen to it that Amanda's refrigerator and cupboards were stocked.

'Since you don't have a car, it is going to be hard to manage groceries,' Cora had told the younger woman.

'Yes, I'll have to work something out,' Amanda had replied. Surely not a major problem. Someone must pass on the highway who could give her a lift. If not, a taxi. Though was Timber large enough for such a service? And how would she call for one when there was no phone in the cabin? Oh, well, time enough to worry about that later. If the worst came to the worst, she would have to buy a small car.

It only took a day and a half for Cora Rosefeld to get the structural inspection completed, sign over her house, pack her things and leave for Phoenix. Keeping her part of the deal struck in Gold Country Properties, she had not told her friends or neighbours who had purchased her house, nor the terms of the deal.

Amanda moved in on the afternoon of Cora's departure, immediately plunging into washing windows, sweeping and dusting the cabin from one end to the other. She dropped into bed when darkness fell, tired, but pleased with her accomplishments. The cabin was clean and tidy, ready for the redecoration project when she decided to get started. But not right away, not just yet. First she'd relax. She slept soundly, not at all disturbed by it being her first night alone in an unfamiliar place. Now she was up and ready for her first day as a home-owner.

Amanda showered and dressed in an old mis-shapen T-shirt, no bra, and jeans. Padding into the kitchen barefoot, she prepared herself a cup of coffee and some toast.

Breakfast ready, she carried it out to the veranda. Pulling one of the tattered plastic folding chairs to the railing, she sat gingerly down, putting her feet on the railing, tilting back. The chair held.

The Ponderosa pines towered over her, rising thirty, forty feet or more into the clear blue of the California sky. She looked up at the dark green branches, silhouetted against the pale blue background, swaying gently in a breeze not felt at ground level. A strong peace invaded Amanda. She drew another deep breath of contentment, of her joy in the day, and sipped her coffee.

Idly she wondered if the track to her place branched from the main drive to the infamous Mac's house.

How far away was this neighbour, the man who owned all the land surrounding her? She had not noticed any lights last night. The countryside had been particularly dark to a girl more used to city street lights, lots of buildings, cars driving by. It had been a long time since she had been so far from the bustle of cities.

Another day I'll follow the drive and find out. But not today. Today is just to sit around and relax and enjoy the trees. She smiled again. If her friends could see her, they would marvel. To sit around and gaze at trees was not their idea of fun.

Amanda munched her toast, eyes roaming here and there, constantly discovering new pleasures in the scene before her. Through the trees, opposite the main drive, she thought she glimpsed another small meadow. Later she'd explore it. She could differentiate between several of the different types of trees, pine, cedar, madrone, but not all. A book on plants would be something to invest in, to learn more about all the flora on her property.

The sun shifted, moving from behind some of the trees, shining its rays directly on the veranda, now, raising the temperature dramatically. As she took another sip of her coffee, Amanda realised her legs were beginning to feel the intense heat of the sun as the dark denims drew the hot rays. Maybe she'd change into shorts. Sunbathe, maybe take a nap. Good grief, getting up so late, and now a nap! It was wonderful!

The hum of a motor penetrated the stillness. At first she was unable to determine from whence it came, then pinpointed it. From further up the driveway. She remained seated, she would change later. If someone from Mac's place were going to drive by, she wanted to see them. She wiggled bare toes in the sun, waiting.

A battered, faded pick-up truck pulled into view but, instead of continuing on to the highway, turned into her track, bouncing on the ruts, driving almost up to the cabin steps. Amanda was fascinated. She had not seen such a dilapidated truck in many years. It had once been a silvery grey, but was now faded, dented and rusted. It was difficult to assign a colour to it now. Piled in the back was a partial bale of hay and a tangle of baling wire. She wondered how it could hold together. Maybe the wire was for repairs.

It ground to a stop, the air suddenly silent.

A tall, powerfully built man climbed out, cowboy hat pulled low on his face, jeans low on his hips. He glanced at the cabin, contemptuously dismissing Amanda after one glimpse, now looking towards the door expectantly as he climbed the steps.

Wow! was Amanda's first impression, followed almost immediately by, you arrogant male! He moved smoothly, swiftly up the stairs, an air of definite purpose about him. At least six feet tall, well-built with broad shoulders, muscular arms, chest straining at the buttons of his checked shirt.

As he reached the veranda, she brought her feet down, stood up. Time to make this visitor aware of her.

'Can I help you?' she asked, turning towards him.

'No.' His eyes raked her, dismissed her.

Amanda was suddenly very aware of her apparel, of her lack of bra, of bare feet. Anger coursed through her at his look. Who did he think she was? She could dress however she chose in her own home.

Indolently, Amanda moved her eyes over him, lifted her head and moved closer. It was the last thing she wanted to do. She'd rather run to the back, out to the yard, anywhere to avoid this man altogether.

'I'm here to see Cora.'

'She's not here.' Amanda did not expand on the statement, facing him defiantly.

'When will she be back?' he asked, fully turning his

attention to her. His voice was low and hard as he faced her. Amanda had heard of people with green eyes, but never actually met anyone with them before. His were a clear green, gazing down at her with contempt. She tilted her head consideringly. If he didn't have a constant frown of disapproval, causing the deep furrows between his eyes and along his mouth, he'd be absolutely smashing.

She took a breath, looked up into his face. She'd been wrong about his size, he must be four inches or more over six feet. She herself was tall, yet had to look up a long way. She wished she had on high-heels.

'She won't be back. She moved to Arizona.'

'Moved!' He was startled. Narrowing his eyes he regarded her as if she were something distasteful. 'When?'

'She left yesterday.'

Suddenly Amanda knew. It had to be, and she didn't blame Cora at all. This man asked to have people against him.

'You must be Mac,' she said, anticipating how angry he'd be upon learning Cora had sold out, and not to him. Served him right.

'Yes. Who are you?'

'Mandy Smith. I'm living here now.'

'Timber's own resident layabout hippie?' he said, glancing again along the length of her, his eyes resting a second longer than necessary on her breasts, outlined by the thin cotton T-shirt, moving, ending with her bare feet.

It was Amanda's turn to be startled, and then amused. Is that how he saw her? A hippie? Just because she had on old clothes, with bare feet and her hair in a braid? She couldn't help smiling. If Mr High-and-mighty only knew. She was not a layabout. She had worked very hard to be where she was. Of course, he might not think she had come so far, worn clothes, run-down cabin. She shrugged.

'Cora's gone,' she repeated. Why had he come?

'To Julie's, I suppose.'

Was that the name she had heard? 'Yes, I think so.'

'Leaving you here until she can sell? Or does she plan to plague me with a stream of undesirable tenants to jack up the price? If she thinks that technique will work, she has another think coming. Damn it!' He spun around without waiting for an answer, pausing only for a moment by the truck for a final, disparaging look at Amanda standing at the top of the steps. He opened the door, climbed in and drove off, gravel spinning beneath his wheels.

Amanda could follow the truck's progress towards the highway until the motor faded from the air. For several moments she continued staring down the drive, reviewing in her mind her meeting with the infamous Mac. What an unpleasant man, for all he absolutely radiated sex appeal. Briefly she toyed with the picture of a different meeting. Her own part vastly changed, the cabin all repaired and decorated, charming and attractive; herself in a fashionable dress, make-up flawless . . . She gave a short laugh. *His* part she could not envisage differently.

'Oh, well.' She shrugged, turning back to the house. She had met Mac and survived. Even experienced a small degree of smugness that he would so quickly jump to an erroneous conclusion, just on her appearance. Now what could she do to justify his opinions? Ideas crowded her head, a small joy at the thought of leading him on.

As she went to change, Amanda dwelt less on the visit than on the man himself. He was extremely good-looking in a rugged sort of way. Skin the colour of teak, eyes startling in his brown face. She remembered how his jaw tightened when he heard Cora had gone, his cheeks slightly hollow, cheekbones high. She wondered if his hair was dark or not. She had not noticed it because of his hat. His body was trim and fit, evidence of hard work and temperate living. What did he do for a living, she wondered. Probably a rancher. Timber lay in the heart of mountain ranch land. If he owned all the land surrounding her place, it followed his profession was probably tied up in it. His attitude needed improvement, though. His constant frown would be wearing. She didn't envy his wife, having to live with his constant disapproval. Of course, he might not disapprove of her.

Quickly Amanda donned a pair of shorts and a brief top. Taking a blanket from the bed, she stretched out on her verandah, legs and arms exposed to the sun. She knew better than to stay out too long; the air was thinner at these heights, affording less protection from the sun's rays. Gradually she relaxed, letting her thoughts drift, fully at ease in the heat of the day. Conscious of the time, she turned over, then dozed for a little while.

The hum of the pick-up truck brought her awake as it raced up the drive. She opened sleepy eyes and watched through the railing posts as it passed. Aware of the warmth of her skin, Amanda rose and went inside.

Two days later Amanda decided she was ready to explore her new environs. Dressed in the inevitable jeans and cotton top, she walked down her track to the main drive. Left to the highway? Or right to see where Mac lived? Her heart sped up a little at the thought of confronting her neighbour again. Maybe another day. She'd opt for the highway now.

It was pleasant walking along the gravel drive, the air clean, scented with pine and cedar. A wonderful change from city pollution. She pushed the tinted glasses up; they had a tendency to slide down her nose.

A hat. That's what she needed. Maybe she could walk to town one day this week and get one. It would shelter her from the hot sun, as well as providing relief from the glare.

Reaching the highway, she turned right, away from town, and ambled along the shoulder of the road, exploring as she walked. The road lay in the sun, with dappled shade in long splotches as the trees sheltered it here and there. The day was warm, but not hot. Now and then Amanda heard a rustle in the undergrowth. She would stop quickly, peering in the direction of the sound, trying to see what it was. The only animals she saw, however, were the grey squirrels in the trees. She looked in vain for a deer. How complete the walk would be if she could sight one.

A slight dip in the highway and Amanda came to a bridge spanning a large creek. Water tumbled over rocks and rushed around large bleached boulders as it scurried on its way to the sea. She stopped to watch the water. Its melody was pleasant, soothing. The rapids and eddies mesmerising. Why was the sound of water so soothing, so peaceful? For many long minutes she stood and watched, lost in thought.

Rousing herself at last, Amanda left the road to follow the stream up for a short distance. She suspected it might even be the one that crossed her property and, if it were, she could follow it home. It was easy to walk along the bank; the ground was not particularly steep, nor overgrown, the gurgle and splashes of the tumbling water a wonderful background sound as she moved deeper into the forest. The words and melody of a new song began forming in her head. When she reached home, she'd try them out with her guitar. Repeating the phrases over and over, she wished she had brought pen and paper. Still, by repeating it enough, she wouldn't forget. An entire verse fell into place. She tried humming a little of the melody: it would work. It sounded good.

Softly she sang the words to the tune, over and over. That would have to do until she could put it down permanently on paper.

As if awakening from a dream, she stopped suddenly and took stock of where she was. She had wandered a long distance from the highway. Directly before her was another bridge, a wooden one this time. It looked old and somehow not substantial enough to bear any weight. She climbed up from the stream bank to stand on the planking. The road leading to it was gravelled, not paved.

Oh, oh, she thought. From behind her came the roar of a familiar engine.

Resignedly she stood her ground as the old, grey pick-up rounded the bend, slowing to a stop at the bridge's edge.

'You're trespassing,' came a voice she knew.

Walking up to the window on the driver's side, she replied, 'I know. I was following the stream up from the highway.'

The green eyes studied her. His jaw had not relaxed. Amanda's spirits sank.

'I didn't bother anything,' she said quietly.

'Never said you did,' was the reply. 'Get in and I'll take you up to the house. I have something to talk to you about.'

Why not? She walked around to get into the truck. It might be interesting to see where the dreaded Mac lived. She smiled at her fancy. Dreaded Mac indeed. He was only a bad-tempered, cross old man. Well, she corrected herself, not so old either, maybe thirty-five or so.

She slammed the door and they started. The bridge creaked ominously to Amanda's ear, but Mac seemed unconcerned. Once safely across, she looked eagerly about her as the drive continued through the forest, climbing gently.

'You on something?' he asked.

'What?' She swung her gaze to him.

'Pot smokers and drug addicts wear sunglasses all the time to protect their eyes from the sun.'

'Well, I'm not on anything!' she snapped. 'Millions of people also wear sunglasses just to cut the sun's glare.'

'Yes.' He did not sound convinced.

Amanda gave him a hard look. Gone was the tranquillity, the exhilaration she had felt on her walk, the delight with the new song. Oh, drat the man, he was irritating!

The truck ground up a final, steep rise, coming to rest on the plateau before a large house.

Amanda sat spellbound. The house was rambling, with lots of glass. There was no question why: the view was breathtaking. The land fell away on the far side of the house, to open up the view for endless miles. Tree-covered mountain after tree-covered mountain rose in the distance, a bluish haze blurring their outlines, blurring, but by no means obliterating. In the far distance, lofty snow-capped peaks raised their heads, gleaming brightly against deep blue sky. Amanda was breathless with the beauty of it.

'Come on in, I'll get you a drink or something.' Mac got out and waited in front of the truck for her to join him.

Amanda reluctantly opened her door. She would much rather just drink in this view. It was fantastic! She had heard the Sierra Nevada range was considered one of the loveliest mountain ranges in the world. Vistas like this one would certainly reinforce that opinion.

Meekly she followed Mac into his house, vaguely aware of music as they approached the door. Opening it, Mac muttered something and strode in ahead of her.

It was the first time outside of a rehearsal hall or review session that Amanda had heard herself sing on a record. She cocked her head, smiling, listening. It wasn't bad.

'Shut that thing off!' Mac roared, slapping his hand on one of the doors leading from the main room.

Almost immediately, the sound diminished. Diminished, but was not extinguished.

Amanda looked at Mac with surprise. Was it the song he disliked, or music in general? Maybe just the volume. It had been loud.

Mac continued to the back of the room, pausing to glance back at Amanda still by the front door.

'You can move, you know. What do you want to drink?'

She bristled at his comment. Graciousness obviously was not one of his traits. 'Coke,' she replied.

When he left the room, she exhaled a sigh of relief. Why was she so uptight in his presence? Granted, he rubbed her up the wrong way, but that was no reason to let him get to her. Get hold of yourself, girl, she admonished.

Not letting his remark rankle, she moved slowly into the living room. It was casually furnished, with good quality, rugged pieces. The upholstery on some of the furniture was bold and distinctive, vibrant blues and golds contrasting with the dark, natural wood. It was pleasant and inviting. Amanda thought someone other than the disapproving owner must have decorated it.

She was drawn to the window on the left wall. It was large, wide, overlooking the view she had seen from the truck. Amanda stood in awe. The distant mountains rose to the sky, trees, acres of trees, on the nearer ones. From this vantage point, she realised the land did not drop off abruptly on the far side of the house, but rather gradually descended until it again met the forest. Two fenced fields with horses dozing in the afternoon sun encompassed most of the grassy area before the house. To the far right, she could glimpse a barn.

She heard the firm stride of his step as Mac returned. Turning from the window, she moved to the sofa, watching him warily as he entered the room.

He had a Coke can and glass in one hand, a beer in the other. Seeing her, he raised an eyebrow.

'We're inside now, no sun.' He looked pointedly at her glasses.

Raising her hand, Amanda pushed them firmly up on her nose, not tempted by his taunt. The door on the opposite wall opened and a tall, lanky teenager emerged. Faint strains from another of her recent records wafted out.

'Turn that thing off, can't you?' Mac growled out.

The boy looked at him and smiled cheekily.

'Yeah, but when it's finished. Who's this?' He turned to Amanda. He was tall and very thin, with reddish hair and pale blue eyes. Amanda judged him to be near sixteen years of age, but couldn't be sure. She was not particularly good at guessing ages.

'I'm Mandy Smith.' She stood and held out her hand.

'Probably made up,' he replied, winking at her, grasping her hand in a firm handshake.

'Is that what you think?' Amanda was surprised. Good heavens, he was as bad as Mac!

'Not me,' he protested laughing.

Amanda spun to Mac. 'Is that what *you* think, then?' When he made no reply, she continued, 'At least I gave you a name. I don't know yours.'

'You do, you said it the other day at Cora's.'

'Mac, that's all, and I guessed that. Don't you have another? A first, or last?'

'Oh boy, that's good! So much for teaching me manners, Dad,' the boy jeered.

Dad! This was certainly a day for surprises. Amanda looked from one to the other. Father and son. They didn't look it, except for maybe height. Mac was much more substantial, more rugged. The boy's features, while still youthfully immature, were more finely drawn. She wondered how old Mac was, she would have to revise her estimate. He didn't look older than thirty-five, yet to be the father of this boy . . .

'My apologies, Miss Smith. I'm John MacKensie. This is my son, John-Michael,' Mac replied in an angry voice. Turning to his son, he continued, 'Did you get the stable mucked out like I asked?'

'Yeah, it's done. I'm going to get a Coke. Don't let my old man bully you, Miss Smith.' He smiled at her, swung wide when passing his father, headed to the kitchen.

Mac put the drinks on the table before the sofa. 'Want a glass?'

'No, the can is fine. Do you have any other children, Mr MacKensie?'

He smiled sardonically. 'Mac'll do. I have no intention of calling you Miss Smith for the short time we'll know each other.'

She took a long drink of the Coke, letting the provocative remark slide. What did he want? Why was she here? She glanced at him again, glad for the sunglasses sheltering her a little from him. His presence was overpowering. She needed all the defences she could muster against him.

Mac removed his hat, tossing it on a table near the door, running the fingers of his right hand through the flattened copper-coloured waves. Amanda felt an involuntary stirring of interest. He was devastatingly attractive. She had not noticed his hair before, because of his hat. What a striking combination with his tanned skin and green eyes. Did the man realise it? Was he aware of the sheer animal magnetism he radiated? Amanda did not *like* him, but couldn't help herself wondering what it would be like to be kissed by him, to be held in his arms . . . Stop it! She took a long sip of Coke, forcing her eyes away, forcing her thoughts elsewhere.

He sat in a chair near the sofa, motioning her to resume her seat. Gingerly, she sat on the edge, conscious of the rising tension in the room.

'I won't beat about the bush. I want your property. I thought Cora had let you rent it to torment me, but on checking with Martin Roberts and verifying it in the county records in San Andreas, I find the property now belongs to you. I want it. How much?'

Amanda took another sip. 'It's not for sale,' she said quietly.

John-Michael entered the room with the loose-jointed gait peculiar to teenagers the world over. He paused, looking at his father, then Amanda.

'Did I interrupt something?'

'No.' Amanda took a final sip, putting her can down. 'Your father wanted to talk about buying my land. It's not available, so end of conversation.' To Mac she said, 'Thanks for the drink. See you.'

She rose and smiled at John-Michael. 'I love your taste in music,' she said with secret delight. If he only knew!

Mac also rose, but no smile crossed his face. 'Is that your final word? Not for sale?'

She nodded.

'I think you should reconsider.' Was it a veiled threat?

'You have such a way with words, Mr MacKensie. Is that a threat?'

'No, just advice.'

'I'll keep it in mind. I'm going now. Thanks again for the Coke.'

Amanda moved determinedly to the door. So much

for the MacKensies. She knew he wanted the land, now he knew it was no more available to him than it had been under Cora.

'Goodbye, Miss Smith,' John-Michael called.

'Bye.'

Amanda was a hundred yards down the drive before she realised she had not met Mrs MacKensie. Nor, come to that, even heard her mentioned. Was she away? Or was there no Mrs MacKensie? She shrugged. What did it matter? She would probably not see much of the MacKensies.

She paused once again to let her eyes take in the beautiful view, a quick glance at the modern house, and she set off for home, drawing peace and strength from the serenity of the land she was passing through. Soon the words to the song crowded her head again. Amanda quickened her step. She wanted to write them down before they faded from her mind.

CHAPTER THREE

AMANDA strummed the chord again; again. Now from the beginning. She played the melody more confidently this time, sang the new words softly, under her breath. No, this part still wasn't quite right. Still didn't flow as well as the rest. She tried another string, another chord. She could hear it in her head, why couldn't she get it right on the guitar? It was frustrating.

'Hello.'

Amanda looked up from her concentration to see a horse and rider on the main drive. John-Michael MacKensie, mounted on a large chestnut horse.

'Hi, come on over,' she invited, putting the guitar aside. She pushed her glasses on her nose, turned the paper over and watched as John-Michael rode up, dismounted and tied his horse to a post of the railing.

'I didn't know if you'd be home or not,' he said, joining her on the veranda. He was already over six feet tall. Amanda wondered if, when he had filled out, he would approach his father's size.

'Especially to a MacKensie.'

'Why not to a MacKensie? I only know two of them and one I think I could like.' Amanda smiled. 'Have a seat.'

'You play the guitar?' he asked, picking it up and strumming a few times.

'Yes, do you?'

'No, don't play any instrument. I'd like to, though. I can sing a little. Is it hard to learn?'

'No, it's not. I could start you off, if you like. Much of it is self-taught, if you stick with it, practise every day. Do you have one?'

'I could pick one up in town. When can we begin?' He strummed again, then looked up eagerly.

'Now.' Amanda rose, came around and stood behind him, positioning his hands, placing his fingers in the correct position on the strings.

'These three fingers on these three strings, thus,' she pressed the fingers, 'are the C chord. Now strum.' John-Michael did so several times, nodding his head.

'Now,' she rearranged the fingers, 'try that; it's G.'

He did, his face lighting up with pleasure. 'I can hear the difference. I'm playing!' He continued to play C and G, alternating back and forth, strumming fast, now slowly, a look of pure happiness on his face.

Amanda sat back and watched him, remembering back to when she had first learned, the excitement she had felt, the joy of actually making music. She still experienced some of that each time she played and sang. Love of music is not something one outgrows.

He stopped and looked up, sheepishly shaking his left hand. 'It's a bit of a strain.'

'Yes, but only until you are used to it.'

John-Michael handed the guitar to her. 'Play something for me, please.'

Amanda hesitated. She was serious in her desire to spend some time away from the crowds and people who knew her as a popular country singer. Yet she had no wish to deny John-Michael's simple request. What could she sing that would not give her away? Dozens of songs filled her head, most of which she had recorded at one time or another.

She began strumming, then singing. Her husky voice swelling and carrying ... 'Go tell it on the mountains ...'

John-Michael watched her fingers as she moved through the song, the different strings she pressed as the chords changed. When Amanda finished, she launched into a fast paced melody with fingers racing.

It was a difficult piece, ideal for limbering up fingers. She knew she was showing off, but couldn't resist. It wasn't often she had such an appreciative audience of one.

'Bravo!' John-Michael exclaimed, applauding, when she finished.

'Not bad,' a nearby voice drawled.

The couple on the veranda turned to see Mac quietly sitting on a large bay beside the other horse. Engrossed in Amanda's song and music, neither had noticed him ride up.

'Not too bad. You ought to try to get a job somewhere,' Mac said, his eyes holding hers.

A hot retort arose in Amanda's throat, but she kept it in. Blast the man, if he wanted to see her as a hippie, far be it from her to disabuse him of the notion. She shrugged. 'Just waiting for my big break,' she said, bending her head to the guitar.

'Thought you were riding to Murphy's,' Mac addressed his son.

'Well, I just stopped off here for a few minutes first. Mandy's going to teach me how to play the guitar.'

'For a properly large fee, I'm sure.'

John-Michael turned a questioning face towards Amanda, but she spoke before he could say anything.

'For fun, Mr Cynic.'

'Few women do anything for fun without it costing others.'

'And what is that supposed to mean?'

'Nothing, Mandy,' John-Michael spoke up hastily. 'Dad's mad because my mother ran off with Cora's son. He doesn't like women much.'

Amanda's head jerked round to Mac MacKensie as his son spoke. No wonder he disapproved of women, a natural reaction to his wife's defection. But how had the woman been able to leave him? He was one of the most attractive men Amanda had come across, his rugged good looks, the stuff dreams were made of. His confidence and self-assurance were traits most women admired and wanted in a man. Sitting nonchalantly on the big bay, he was a man to be reckoned with, to learn to deal with, to grow to know and trust, not run away from.

'No need to air dirty linen in public,' Mac said.

John-Michael flushed. 'Mandy's not like that. I'm grateful to her for offering to teach me,' he mumbled defiantly.

Mac gave her a long, hard look before turning back to his son. 'You get along to Murphy's.' Without another word, he wheeled his horse around and rode quickly away, up the drive, towards the large house at the summit. Amanda watched him leave with a sudden, unexplained feeling of loss, her eyes still on the drive long after he had disappeared.

'When would be a good time for lessons?' John-Michael asked diffidently as he rose and moved towards the steps.

She smiled kindly at the tall boy. 'You need to practise between sessions. If you don't have a guitar, you can come use this one. Any time is fine, except mornings. I like my mornings to myself.'

'OK.' He moved down the stairs, untied his horse. 'I'll see about the guitar.' Swinging himself up, he said, 'I'll be down again. Thanks, Mandy.'

She sketched a small wave as he turned his horse and started off, presumably for Murphy's.

The afternoon seemed empty now. She stared at the music, but the burning desire to capture the words and melody had faded. Later, or tomorrow, she'd work on it again, but now the urge was gone.

A general lassitude overtook her as she tilted her chair back to sit in the sun and enjoy the gentle breeze skipping across the veranda. Ruminating on the revelation of John-Michael, she wondered at the circumstances of Mac's marriage, of its ending. Would she ever know? Probably not; the summer was too short, and it was not her style to pump others for information. Interesting thought, though.

Amanda awoke with a sense of purpose the next morning. She was going to walk into town this day and see what arrangements she could make for obtaining groceries on a regular basis. Maybe she'd also get a hat today. The sun was fierce at these higher elevations and she could use the protection one afforded.

Having straightened up the cabin, but a few moments' work, she sat down to make a list. While she could not purchase all she wanted today, she could at least determine what she needed, and decide what to get today, what she would be able to carry back.

Groceries. That was easy: jot down things she liked and the things she was low on. Toiletries. Now, cushions or large pillows to use in the living room until she could get furniture. A rug, a few knick-knacks for the place. A few inexpensive items would go a long way to brightening up the area until she could begin the real work of painting and decorating. She didn't recall seeing a furniture store in town. She would probably have to get furniture from a larger city. Time enough for that later. There was no rush.

A radio. She also wanted a radio, battery powered, so she wouldn't be so cut off. Relaxing was one thing, being totally isolated was something else again. A telephone was also needed. She would make arrangements for one when she was in town, too. Cora really led a reclusive life, without many of the conveniences Amanda took for granted.

The list ready, she hitched up her shoulder bag, placed her glasses firmly on her nose and set off. It was just past mid-morning. She hoped the day would not prove too hot, but knew it would only be worse later on.

The walk proved pleasant. The air was clean and scented, balmy and soft against her skin. The shoulder of the highway was graded and easy to walk on. Two or three cars passed her, but the traffic on the highway was not heavy. Winding down the hill to Timber, Amanda reminded herself that the walk back would be uphill the entire way. Even more reason to exercise constraint when shopping.

She heard another vehicle from behind her, but did not turn. Time enough to see it when it passed.

It didn't. Slowing, it pulled off the road, stopping just behind her.

'Going to town?'

Amanda turned. Mac MacKensie had stopped.

'Yes, I have some shopping to do.'

'Climb in. I'm going in and will give you a lift.'

'Thanks.' No false pride for Mandy Smith. It was a long walk and if she could cover the distance in a fraction of the time, so much the better.

'What are you going to buy?' he asked as she settled in and slammed the door. The truck started again.

'Some groceries. And a hat, maybe.'

He threw her a look. 'Good idea; get a grey one, sort of silvery. I bet you'd look nice in silver.'

Amanda stared at him. Could she believe her eyes? Mac MacKensie almost friendly, almost complimentary? Giving a suggestion in a pleasant manner, no order. She was surprised he had even considered such a thing as what colour she would look good in.

Her mind jumped to the silvery outfit she wore sometimes when performing. Would Mac think she looked nice in that?' It showed her figure to advantage, was a colour that flattered her. For a moment she tried to imagine what Mac's reaction to her in the silver outfit would be. How he would smile, take her in his arms, press his mouth against her throat, her lips . . .

Amanda jerked her head round, staring out the window. What could she be thinking of? Good heavens, anyone would think her a love-struck teeny-bopper! Granted, she found Mac incredibly attractive physically, but she had been around attractive men before, without this reaction. She had better watch it. Was she getting bored already? Already fantasising to pass the time? Looking for a summer romance? No. Then why the daydreams?

Mac drew the truck to a halt near the bus depot. Amanda looked around, already recognising places in town.

'My business here should take about an hour. If you're ready to go back then, I'll give you a lift,' Mac said as he turned off the engine. 'If not, you're on your own.'

'Fair enough, thanks.'

He nodded.

Amanda's first stop was Murphy's, Timber's one department store. She smiled when she recognised the name. This was where John-Michael had been heading yesterday. She selected a bright rug and four large upholstered pillows in harmonising patterns and colours of blue and green. One or two bright accessories would complete her venture into temporary decorating for the day. It would be a bit Bohemian but, since she was the only one living there, what did it matter? She liked it. It would suffice until she could get to all the ideas she had for redecorating.

She wandered to the clothing section. Trying on several hats, she did finally settle on one in a silvery grey. What a sucker for a man's suggestion, she jeered herself, as she paid the sales clerk. Would he even comment on it? Even notice it?

One last item, the small radio, and she was ready.

Gathering her packages, she could scarcely hold them all and manoeuvre through the aisles. Pushing her way outside, Amanda made her way to the truck. As she was well within her hour, she did not expect to find Mac there. With a swift glance up and down the street, she determined it would be safe to leave her purchases in the rear of the pick-up, as long as she didn't mind a little straw and hay when she got home.

She dropped the packages in and looked around. Seeing a likely store, she went to make enquiries about the phone. She was disappointed to find it would take longer to instal than she had anticipated, but they would have it in by the end of the month. An appointment was made and she proceeded to the market.

It was well after the hour's time when she finally finished grocery shopping. The truck was still parked where Mac had left it when she came out, laden with two large bags and one smaller one gripped tightly in her hand. Hurriedly she moved along the pavement. Don't let him start off just now, she thought, not when I'm so close.

Drawing nearer, she saw Mac leaning against the bonnet, talking to another man on the pavement. With a sigh of relief, she slowed her pace a little. The two men noticed her at the same time. Mac pushed off and came to meet her, taking two of the bags.

'Thank you.' Amanda smiled warmly in her relief. She could not have carried the bags all the way home.

He glinted down at her. 'You're late.' Disapproval back.

'I know. Thank you for waiting.' She dumped the third bag into the back of the truck, not letting his bad temper affect her.

'It's a good thing I did wait,' he replied, putting in the other bags. 'How would you have managed for the five miles or so to your place?'

She smiled impishly. 'I would have coped. Do you like my hat?' she said, changing the subject.

For a moment Amanda thought she saw a softening of his features; no, she must have imagined it. He was as impassive, as disapproving as ever. With no reply, he took her arm and led her over to the man he had been talking with.

'Ed Tyler, I'd like you to meet Mandy Smith. She lives in Cora's place.'

'How do you do?' Amanda shook hands. Ed Tyler was tall and very thin, with a weathered face and kind eyes.

'Pleased to meet you, Miss Smith. I did hear Cora had left us. Glad you've come to settle here. We don't get a lot of young blood moving into Timber. Most young folks want big cities and excitement.' He smiled kindly at Amanda, then turned back to Mac.

'Keep in mind what I said. Let me know if you think of something.'

'I will.' Mac shook hands and bade him goodbye. As Ed ambled away, Mac opened the door for Amanda.

'Ready now?'

She gave him a look as she climbed in. No one had asked him to wait. Though she was very glad he had.

Fifteen minutes later they were unloading the truck, carrying in the bags and packages to Amanda's cabin. Mac had not said anything on the ride, nor spoken when they reached her place. He got out of the cab and began unloading the supplies. He followed Amanda in, made two more trips. Putting down the last package, he looked around.

'Looks about the same as when Cora had it.'

'Yes, I know. But that's what is in some of the packages, things to brighten it up a little, until I can get it painted and get some rugs and furniture.'

'Mandy, I want you to listen to my offer. I know from the county records what the place sold for. I can give you a nice profit on it.' He shook his head and held up one hand as she made to speak.

'No, just listen. I also know from chatting with Martin Roberts that you just stumbled across this place. I'm sure that there are others around here that would be just as good. I want this property.'

'It's not for sale,' she replied. He was stubborn, but she could be also.

'Times will get rougher when the mortgage comes due. Work is scarce around here. I don't know how you financed it to start with . . .'

'I wrote a cheque,' she tossed off flippantly.

'Sure you did. You have to keep up with a mortgage. Then there are taxes, assessments . . .'

'If it is such a burden,' she interrupted, 'why do you want it so much?'

'It's MacKensie land. My father deeded this portion over to Cora Rosefeld years ago. It was a mistake. I want it back.'

'No sale.'

'Dammit, Mandy,' he slammed a fist down on her table, 'you have all of Calavaras County out there. Find another place. I'll pay any increase within reason.'

'Another place won't be so appealing, won't have a stream; won't have bluebells on the hill.'

'You can *plant* flowers!' he roared.

'It's not the same!'

He shook his head wearily and moved towards the door.

'Mac.' Amanda stopped him. 'Thank you for taking me to town, and for waiting. It was most kind and helpful.'

He paused and looked back at her, a grin lighting his face, the first Mandy had seen on him. What a change; he looked younger, happier almost.

'Maybe I'll get to you with kindness. See you.'

She remained where he left her, staring thoughtfully after him. When had his wife left him? Amanda didn't think it had been recently, not if the lines on his face were an indication. They were too deep; too set not to be from years of frowning. Were they divorced, or just separated? Had they tried a reconciliation? She smiled, trying to visualise knowing him well enough to ask. She couldn't ever envisage such a time. Still, if he were planning to 'get her with kindness', she could try to make him smile more. What a challenge that might be.

Amanda turned to her purchases. She reached up to remove her hat, then paused. Walking to the bathroom, she peeked at herself in the mirror. Cora Rosefield certainly could not have been a vain woman, the sole mirror in the cabin was the one over the bathroom sink. What Amanda saw when she peered in pleased her. The pale grey hat was attractive, its silvery colour bringing a glow to her skin. Her blue eyes seemed deeper, her skin smoother. Tipping it down over one eye, she tried for a seductive look. Pushing it flat back gave her an open, friendly look. She giggled, tilting her head to one side. Which mood would work best with Mr Mac MacKensie?

Tiring of her game, she returned to put away her groceries, then turned to her other purchases. She tore the paper from the large cushions, arranging them near the wall. The fresh colours in the cushions only emphasised the dirty, faded condition of the walls. She would have to paint soon. The soft blues and greens brightened the living room, made it prettier already. Two small lacy cushions gave a feminine accent to the rather rugged cabin. Lastly, a small rug, to place before the cushions and, later, before a sofa when she bought one.

She stepped back to admire.

It was almost like Christmas, with all the new

packages, she thought as she drew out the Sony compact radio, with built-in tape player. She inserted the batteries according to the directions, tuning in to a local station. The gentle strains of the music filled the room, making it at once more comfortable. A home, now, no longer just a cabin in the woods.

As the radio played softly in the background, Amanda drew the last purchase from its wrapper, a large sloping-sided black pan, with ridges along one side. A pan to use in searching for gold: the black colour to facilitate spotting the golden flakes or nuggets, the ridges to offer resistance for the heavier metal when the water washed out the sand and grit of lighter materials. Tilting and swishing, she tried to practise what the salesgirl had shown her, a small smile of happiness on her lips as she pretended she was already panning for gold.

Tomorrow she'd go up to her creek on her hill, near her bluebells, and try her luck. What fun!

A rap at the door startled her. Glancing around almost guiltily, she quickly stashed the tell-tale pan in the kitchen, out of sight. Going to the door, she found John-Michael, guitar in hand, smiling shyly at her.

'Hi.' He sounded unsure of his welcome.

'Hi, yourself. Time for another lesson?'

'Yes, if you have time.'

'Sure, come on in. I just got back from shopping.'

'I know, you weren't home earlier. I came by. If it's not convenient, I'll come another time. I got a guitar,' he offered shyly.

'I can see, good brand. Come in and sit down. No not there, use one of the chairs; those cushions won't give proper position. Will interfere with your hands and arms. Did you practise what we did the other day?'

'Yes.' John-Michael strummed a few times, changing the chords.

'Good. I'll get my guitar and we'll get started.' Amanda took off her hat, tossing it casually on to the table. She pulled out another chair, turning it so it faced John-Michael, then got her guitar.

'You look kind of familiar, like I've seen you before,' John-Michael commented as Amanda strummed a few chords.

'You have, just a day ago. Let's get started.' She bent her head to look at her guitar. Blast, she had forgotton John-Michael had some of her albums. Her eyes were distinctive enough, even with her hair pulled back and a changed environment, for her to stand out. She should have put the tinted glasses back on. Oh, well, take his mind off it and maybe he'd let it go.

'Now, try these strings; fingers here.' Amanda watched as John-Michael faithfully followed her directions with serious concentration.

'Loosen up, John-Michael,' she urged gently. 'Enjoy it, it's fun.'

He smiled, but became serious again as he changed the chords. In a minute he stopped. 'It hurts your fingertips,' he said, flexing his left hand.

Amanda nodded. 'Yes, initially. But you can build up calluses, see?' She held out her left hand, showing hardened fingertips. When you build these up, you can play forever and your fingers don't bother you.' She shifted position slightly.

'Now, there are other ways to strum.' Amanda demonstrated different rhythms, plucked the strings, and waited each time for John-Michael to try.

'Good,' she praised. 'You can also use a pick but, unless I play a steel string, I prefer to use my own fingers and thumb.'

'You have a steel-string guitar, too?' John-Michael was surprised. 'Electric?' He looked puzzled, as if wondering how someone could have so many instruments.

'Of course,' she replied. Oh, oh, she caught herself, there's no 'of course' about that. It is not an instrument that just everyone has, especially if they already have an acoustic guitar. She began strumming again to avoid further conversation on that topic. There was more to trying to hide an identity than she had bargained for.

Not that the world would end if the whole town knew who she was, but she did so want to be just plain Mandy Smith for a while, for one summer. Have a place she could be herself, not a country singer.

John-Michael practised his chords, faithfully changing every few strums of his right hand. After ten minutes, he looked up.

'Now do I know enough to do a song?'

'Sure, let's see if I can think up one using only those chords.' Dozens of songs flashed through her mind, but most were too complicated for a beginner. 'How about *Mary Don't You Weep?*'

'OK, sounds good. What to do first?'

'G first, then C then D. Listen and watch my hand.' Slowly Amanda began strumming, her left hand pressing the strings. Softly she sang the song, almost in a monotone.

John-Michael watched, trying his fingers on his guitar, but not strumming. When she had finished he nodded. 'OK, I can try it now.'

Amanda reversed roles this time, fingered the chords without playing the guitar. He stumbled several times, was late in changing a chord, and moved very slowly through the song. Nonetheless, pride in achievement showed in his face when he finished.

'Bravo, John-Michael, very good!' Amanda smiled at his happiness. 'I've thought of another one, too, *Oh, Susannah*. Try it with me. Listen to when the sound changes so we can change chords. We'll be a duo before long.'

'Yeah, do duelling guitars, instead of duelling banjos.'

'Or we could do duelling banjos.'

'You have a couple of banjos?' He was incredulous.

Amanda caught herself this time. No 'of course'; she was cautious in her reply.

'I have access to a couple.'

She could call Dave and get him to send her banjo. She'd better call him, anyway, and let him know where she was, and that she had not forgotten their date in Nashville later in the month. He would not fully approve of her life here. He had found it difficult to understand that she really wanted the summer off, had wanted to leave the city and find a restful, quiet place to relax, to spend the summer. He would be shocked at her buying a house. To footloose, free-living Dave, a house was an awful, permanent, restraining burden. He wanted to be able to up and move when the mood struck, not be tied down with material possessions. Yes, she would have to call him.

'OK, John-Michael, let's try it.'

They played through the song a couple of times, and repeated the first one again before Amanda called a halt.

'You practise those; next time we'll expand your repertoire.'

'OK. Thanks for the lesson.' He flushed, shifted a little in his chair. 'Is there anything I can do to repay you for them?' he asked diffidently.

'No, John-Michael,' she said gently. 'I'm just glad you want to learn. You come on down any time. We can play or learn more, or just visit, if you like.'

'Thanks, Mandy. I'll do it.' He smiled shyly.

For a brief moment, Amanda saw his father's face reflected in the smile. Mac had once been young, carefree and probably had looked a little as his son did now. It was a pity his wife's defection had changed him so much.

CHAPTER FOUR

THE next morning dawned fair and warm. Amanda rushed through breakfast and her cleaning chores so she could try her hand at panning for gold. She was full of anticipation at the prospect and hurried through the dusting and sweeping so she could proceed.

Shortly before ten o'clock, she plopped her hat on her head, grabbed the black pan and headed to her portion of the creek. She wore shorts and a light, sleeveless cotton top, both in a pale blue that complemented her eyes. Her tennis shoes she planned to take off at the water's edge.

Once out of doors, she slowed down, walking steadily, but not rapidly, towards the creek, raising her head to feel the sun. It was already hot on her arms; she was glad for the shelter the hat would provide. She would still have to watch it, the sun was strong at these heights. Amanda smiled with growing happiness at the day's beauty: the expanse of Ponderosa pines, Douglas fir and California cedars soaring in stately dignity, the clear blue sky, and the bluebells nodding in the gentle morning breeze. The soft gurgle of the water could be heard in the air as she drew near the creek.

When she reached it, Amanda paused, trying to determine the best place to begin. She had talked to the woman in the store when buying the pan; basics had been briefly explained, cautions against fool's gold stressed. When she saw a small waterfall of less than three feet, the water cascading over in a steady stream, she moved to try there. The major part of the snowpack from higher up had melted. As the summer wore on, the stream would probably diminish in size until it was no more than a trickle curling its way around the large rocks and boulders scattered in its bed. There were very few spots where the creek bed was sandy, free from rocks.

One look and Amanda elected to keep her shoes on. She had another pair at the cabin and the rocks in the creek looked sharp. They were certainly not smooth pebbles. Gingerly she stepped into the water, heading for the waterfall.

It was like ice!

Well, obviously, she chided herself as she stepped quickly back to the bank. It was melted snow, couldn't be expected to be warm. Equally obvious, she could not stand for hours on end in the numbing cold. No wonder so much gold remained in the California mountains; who could pan for it? They would get frostbite.

Disappointed at not being able to start, she wandered upstream for a few hundred feet, searching for a better spot, one where she could stay dry. She found another likely spot, at the base of still another small cascade, where the heavier gold would probably settle out and down to the bottom during flood season. This particular area had the advantage over the first of having a large, almost flat rock near the base for her to sit on.

Started at last, Amanda found it pleasant to swirl sand and grit from the stream bed in her pan, allowing the water to wash out the lighter material, leaving the heavier gold at the bottom of the black pan. Endless scraping up of the stream bed, swishing it around in the pan, letting the water wash it out over the side, examining heavier grains to see if they were gold. Over and over, Amanda scooped, washed, examined.

Only her tired back forced her to call a halt to her

activities. Judging from the sun's position when she looked up, stretching and rubbing her neck to ease the tightness, it was probably well after noon. She had been at it for over two hours. How quickly the time had flown. Ruefully she watched the water play over the stones. Tomorrow would be another day. She would continue then. The fact that she had not found a single flake or chip she thought was gold did not diminish her enthusiasm. Perhaps she would find some tomorrow. Or the day after.

After a quick lunch, Amanda again set off, this time to walk to Timber. She was going to call Dave, and ask him to send up her banjo. While she was at it, she would reassure him she had not forgotten about their meeting in Nashville in a couple of weeks to discuss a new album with their producer. She dreaded the thought of leaving already, even for a short trip. Still, she couldn't give up her job, either. There were certain responsibilities and tasks to be maintained, even when on holiday.

It was a pleasant walk to Timber, downhill most of the way. Twice cars passed her, heading towards town. Each time her heart skipped a beat. But there was no grey truck stopping to give her a lift this day.

She had to walk the length of Timber, to the bus depot, to the pay phone she remembered was there. Depositing her coins, it was only moments before the phone rang at the other end.

'Hello.' Loud music in the background, almost drowning out the speaker.

'Hi, Dave?'

'Huh? Yes, this is Dave. Hey, you guys, stop a minute, I can't hear.' Gradually the background noise died down.

'This is Dave,' he repeated.

'This is Amanda.'

'Well, where the deuce are you? We haven't heard

one word from you in ages.' As an aside, 'Yes, it's Amanda, be quiet so I can hear her. 'Where are you? Do you realise we are due in Nashville on the 26th?'

'Yes, I know. That's one reason I'm calling. I haven't forgotten about it and will meet you on the 24th, in San Francisco. I have a couple of songs I want your opinion on.'

'Bless me, the girl's gone writing again. Yes, yes, two she says. Amanda, where are you?'

She looked around the small town fondly. 'In a little town called Timber, in Calavaras County.'

There was a silence on the other end.

'Big trees and frogs; whatever are you doing there?'

Amanda giggled at Dave's concept of Calavaras County, the large sequoias and Mark Twain's 'Celebrated Jumping Frog'. 'There's a lot more than just that here. It's a nice area. I like it.'

'Are you in some hotel?'

'No. Dave, I bought a house. And I have a creek and am panning for gold.'

'Bought a house? Are you kidding?'

Amanda could just picture his face. Dave was strictly a city lover, for all he had been raised on a ranch as she had been. His idea of a good place was the thirtieth floor of a big hotel, complete with room service.

'It's old, run down, off the beaten track and glorious!'

He chuckled. 'I can imagine. Better you than me. OK, we'll meet you on the 24th at the St Francis. Don't be late, or I'll have apoplexy.'

'I won't. Can you send me my banjo? I'm giving guitar lessons and said we'd do something with a banjo, too.'

'Good grief, did I hear right? Lessons? Amanda, what are you up to?'

'I'll explain when I see you. Send it care of general

delivery. I have Cora Rosefeld's old place, but don't know if it has an address. I haven't seen a mailman yet.'

'I don't believe it,' Dave said faintly. There was a chorus of voices in the background. 'Later,' Dave hushed them. 'I'm writing this all down, Mandy. I think I have a thousand questions.'

The phone clanged.

'Dave, I've got to go, no more change. Bye.'

'Wait, don't you even have a phone? I thought everyone had a phone these days. How can we get in touch with you?'

'I'll be getting one later. Write to general delivery. I'll call you again. Got to go. Bye.'

Amanda hung up and burst out laughing. She wished she could be there. The speculation would be wonderful. Probably all the background noise had been the rest of the crew, practising, or jamming. Well, she'd see them soon enough, explain then. Though they would probably think she had lost her mind.

Her face sobered. She felt a twinge of homesickness for her friends. She and Dave and Marc and Joe, Phil, Sam, and even Evie. Most of them were related, cousins. All had been friends for years, ever since they had grown up together in Colorado. They had all worked together to put together the production that was 'Amanda'. Except for Evie. Still she fitted right in. Amanda would not be where she was today if not for them all. They enjoyed a special closeness both in work and play and this was the first time she had been away for an extended time since they had started out.

Yet there had to be some time given to other pursuits, Amanda felt. Being a country singer was not all she wanted from life. It was an important part, of course, but surely personal satisfaction, a loving relationship, should be important, too. She wanted to find the right man for her, get married and have children. Not forsaking her career, but combining that and marriage; working when she could, maintain a strong family relationship to return to. She had thought it out and had ideas and plans for a smooth combination when the time came. Until then, she wanted to branch out a little, away from Los Angeles, back to the basics. Time enough for marriage and all when the right man came along. For now, Amanda was satisfied with her career, her new ownership, and her plans for the future.

She walked back up the main street of town, smiling at others as they passed. One or two looked familiar. She had seen them before, though she didn't know their names. One she did know. She stopped to exchange a few words with Martin Roberts when they met.

'Settled in?' he asked.

'Sort of.' She smiled. 'I still have lots to do to fix it up, but it'll keep.'

He shook his head. 'Don't know. I could have found you a fine place, already in tip-top condition.'

'I like my place,' she said gently.

'Um. Mac still wants it, you know. Let me know if I can do anything for you.' He offered his hand.

'Thank you, Martin,' she replied, shaking it firmly.

On impulse, Amanda stopped in Murphy's to tell the friendly clerk about her luck, or lack thereof, in panning for gold. She was welcomed warmly and offered more bits of advice which she promised to follow.

When she drew level with Paul's Pharmacy, Amanda paused. A cold drink would be just right, especially with the long walk ahead of her. It would be more than two hours before she'd reach home.

She pushed open the door. The soda fountain was along the left wall, a lazy ceiling fan giving an illusion of coolness. The establishment was practically deserted.

She had a cold Coke, ignoring the curious glances she received. A stranger in town was always cause for comment. When finished, she wandered across to the book racks and perused the bright covers of the ones on display. If she got one or two, she could take them back to read in the evenings. Being alone was a fine holiday, but sometimes one got just a trifle bored.

Amanda selected three, a mystery, a romance, and a book on plant life in the Sierras. A young girl waited on her, reminding Amanda of the clerk from Murphy's.

'You have Mrs Rosefeld's place now, don't you?' the girl asked as she took the books.

Amanda smiled. 'Yes, that's right. Do you think anyone will ever call it Mandy's place? Or only after I have left?'

The girl giggled at this. 'Probably soon as you leave. That'll be six fifty for the books.'

Amanda set off for home. The walk back wasn't too bad, though more fatiguing than the walk to town had been. Still, the quiet fragrant beauty of the wooded land gave a peaceful air of serenity as Amanda trudged along. The sun was high in the sky, with little shade on the roadside, and no air stirred the limbs of the pines as she made her way uphill.

It was a long, hot walk. Arriving at her cabin, Amanda's first task was a quick shower. She dressed in cool shorts and a brief top, planning only to sit out on the veranda with one of the new books, to enjoy the sun before dinner, soak up the atmosphere of this little area of the country.

Preparing lemonade to take with her, she heard a car door slam. Leaving the glass on the counter in the kitchen, she walked through to the front, picking up her glasses as she passed the table. Through the window she could see a large red car, late model. Who could it be? There came a rap at the door.

Amanda opened it to a slender, elderly, white-haired lady. She was dressed in a cool, lemon dress, and sensible, yet stylish white shoes.

'Hallo,' Amanda said.

'Are you Amanda Smith?' The visitor's voice was rich and pleasant.

'Yes.'

'Well, how do you do? I'm Elizabeth Burke. I've come to welcome you to Timber.'

'How nice. Do come in, unless you'd rather sit on the porch?'

'No, never held with baking in the sun. Dries your skin. Hm. Haven't changed the old place much yet, have you? Nice colours you have added, though. Still, a lot could be done.' Elizabeth Burke entered and made her way regally to a chair. She sat gracefully, fixing her attention on Amanda.

'I confess I was very curious to meet you. I have heard a great deal about you and wanted to see first hand.'

Amanda did not know how to answer that. She moved to sit on another chair, facing her visitor, and waited.

'Well, tell me about yourself,' Elizabeth invited. 'You don't look like a hippie to me, except for those glasses, maybe.'

Amanda made a face. 'You've been talking to Mac MacKensie, I bet. *He* thinks I'm a hippie.'

Elizabeth smiled and nodded. 'Yes to both. He's convinced Cora gave you this place just to plague him. He's wanted it for years, you see.'

'Well, Cora most certainly did not give it to me. I'm sorry he wanted it, but I have it and it is not available for sale.'

Elizabeth's smile grew wider. 'If you talk to him

that way, it's no wonder he gets so fired up discussing you.'

Amanda made no reply but her curiosity seethed. Who was this woman and why was Mac discussing anything with her?

'He's very upset with your presence, you know. But not only because of wanting the property. You are the first woman he has really had to deal with in ages and you don't seem to fall over yourself to please him. Plus, he thinks you are corrupting his son.'

Amanda started to answer when she realised exactly what Elizabeth had said.

'Corrupting his son? How ridiculous. What next? I only offered to teach John-Michael how to play the guitar. Is that corruption?'

'Only if you are a hippie, which Mac thinks you are.' She surveyed the younger woman. 'How do you come to be teaching John-Michael anyway?'

'I was playing one day when he came by. One thing led to another and I agreed to show him the basics.'

Nodding her head, Elizabeth asked, 'And you do play well, don't you?'

'Well enough,' Amanda replied cautiously.

'Yes, and sing, I understand.'

Amanda looked at her warily. 'Does it really matter?'

'Yes. I'm chairman of our Labor Day Festival. We have it each year on Labor Day at the fairgrounds. It's like a big end of the summer party and hospital fund raiser. Each year we have entertainment as part of the programme. The couple we had lined up for this year cannot make it. We just learned of it. It is late in the summer to get anyone, um *big*, you know. I thought perhaps you could sing some songs we all know. We're all friends and neighbours, nothing to get stage fright over.' Elizabeth sat back and waited expectantly.

'I don't know,' Amanda said, reluctant to even

entertain the notion. This was to be her vacation, not a busman's holiday.

'Tickets are sold and proceeds go to our little hospital. It's a good cause, as well as being a part of the town's end of summer tradition.'

'Maybe John-Michael will progress enough to do something,' Amanda said.

'Oh, no, we want more than that. Besides, Mac won't go near the festival, nor let John-Michael. That's when his wife ran off, you know. No, Mac won't permit that.'

Amanda was startled. 'During a festival she ran off?'

'During the festival. Yes. Liza ran off with Cora's son. He had come back that year to visit Cora. It was the year he was one of the performers. We had a small group of actors that year. He's an actor, you know.'

Amanda was fascinated. She slowly shook her head. 'I don't know.'

'Yes, Liza, her name was Elizabeth, same as mine, but she always wanted to be called Liza. And Doug, Cora's son. They met and his life was so much more exciting to her than a rancher's. So they left together. Right before the show. Left us quite in the lurch. Short notice and all.'

Amanda was growing bewildered, trying to follow Elizabeth's monologue. Who was left in the lurch, the programme, or Mac?

'Oh, well, that's a long time ago, now. This will be our fourteenth annual event. Liza left at number two.'

'Mac's been alone for twelve years?' Amanda said, surprised. He must have loved this Liza a great deal to have remained single, devoted to her memory, for so long. Was he still hoping she would return, that they could start again together?

'Well, yes. Doesn't like women much.' Elizabeth shook her head sadly. 'He tolerates me because I'm his aunt, but he really doesn't have any time for women. Pity, but there it is.'

Another surprise. His aunt. Amanda was beginning to feel like Alice at the tea party.

'I didn't realise you were Mac's aunt.'

'Of course. His mother was my sister, you know. I think Mac tolerates me for her sake.' She sighed gently. 'He's kind to me, which is often more than I can say about his boy. He doesn't always treat John-Michael well. I guess it is difficult to raise a child all by yourself.'

'Did his wife not want to have custody of the child?' Amanda asked. These days it was becoming more and more common for the father to gain custody of his children when families separated, but not twelve years ago.

'No. Being a mother was not what Liza wanted. I think that was the major factor in her leaving. She had had enough. Mac thought differently, but who's to say. But I digress. It is this year's festival I must work on. Will you play and sing for us?'

'I might be able to,' Amanda replied, still reluctant to commit herself. 'May I let you know?'

'Yes, I suppose so. I do hope you will. It will be such a relief. I was hoping to hear today, but as soon as you let me know will have to do. John-Michael says you have a good voice, and Mac said you excelled in playing the guitar. I'm sure you could find songs to sing, maybe a dozen or so? It would not be too arduous and would be such a help.'

Amanda smiled. 'We'll see.'

'I'll be satisfied with that,' Elizabeth Burke said.

A shadow fell in the doorway. 'Satisfied with what?' a deep voice asked.

Amanda looked up to find green eyes glittering down on her.

'Hello, Mac,' Elizabeth said, turning in her chair to see her nephew standing in the open doorway.

'I didn't hear your truck,' Amanda commented. 'Did you walk down?'

He shook his head slowly, and entered. 'No, I was going up the drive and saw Elizabeth's car. Wondered what she was doing here.'

'Well, after you and John-Michael told me how well Amanda sings and plays the guitar, it occurred to me she might be able to help out for the festival. Since the Renaldis can't come, I was asking Amanda to sing for us,' Elizabeth explained.

Amanda watched Mac as Elizabeth explained, but the name 'Amanda' appeared to have no special meaning for him. Oddly, she felt a little piqued that he didn't draw a connection between her name and the fact that she sang. So much for her fame preceding her.

Mac glanced derisively at Amanda. 'Could you put on a show for the whole town?' he asked. 'Plan it out and carry it through?' His look raked her, 'layabout hippie' echoing in the air.

The last three words brought a determined lift to Amanda's chin. 'Of course I could.' She paused a moment. Don't let him provoke you, she cautioned herself. More calmly, she continued,

'I have done a show or two before. I play with a few others, actually. We have a small band and ... and play for people.' She finished lamely. It was true. She played with her back-up band sometimes, usually just for fun now, rarely any more at a performance. But when they had started, she had played.

'A band?' Elizabeth's face lit up. 'Wonderful! Could they come and play too? Oh, Mac, that would be grand entertainment, don't you think?'

'I think that's your concern, Elizabeth. I don't hold much with the festival.'

'It wasn't the festival's fault Liza ran off,' she snapped back. 'Doug Rosefeld was in and out all the time to see Cora. Liza was taken with his charm and carefree attitude towards life. You were always so serious. It was just unlucky they went off together at the festival.'

Mac's lips tightened, but he made no reply.

'How's John-Michael?' Amanda tactfully changed the subject.

'Wasting his time fooling with that guitar,' he said, turning his displeasure back on her.

'He might become good at it,' Amanda offered, not intimidated by his attitude.

'So what? So he can drop out of life and play all day like some damned hippie?'

'Doug was not a hippie. Vulgar term,' Elizabeth said. 'He was an actor. Lived a rather Bohemian existence, granted. But, please, Mac, no *hippie*.'

Amanda widened her eyes. Was that the basis of Mac's animosity towards her? Her lifestyle, or what he knew of it, reminded him of the man his wife had run off with? Interesting sidelight.

'John-Michael might become a musician. That's a respectable field.' Just because a person lived a different lifestyle did not make them a hippie.

'Maybe, but it's not much of a moneymaking field, or one that offers stability or job growth. I don't know anyone that makes a decent living at it, do you?'

'Yes, I do,' Mandy replied instantly. 'I know several people who make a very good living from it.' Me for one, she wanted to say.

Mac looked sceptical. 'I just hope it is a passing fad and John-Michael will lose interest before long.'

'It probably won't hurt him,' Elizabeth said, rising gracefully from the old chair. 'I must be going. It's been a pleasure meeting you, Amanda. I do hope you will sing in our festival and persuade your friends in the band to join us. Let me know.'

'I will let you know soon, Mrs Burke.' Amanda rose

to escort her guest to the door. Mac remained standing solidly where he was.

'Bye, Aunt Elizabeth,' he said as she passed.

'Goodbye, dear boy. Give my regards to John-Michael.'

Amanda waved her off from the veranda, before returning to the cabin. Mac had remained where she had left him.

'Did you want something?' she asked rather ungraciously, as he made no move to depart.

He looked rather pointedly at her shorts, displaying her long shapely legs, just beginning to show a tan. He started to say something, then paused, meeting the defiant stare in Amanda's eyes.

'I just wanted to make my views clear as regards John-Michael and his guitar. I don't mind if he learns. It will give him something to do. I will object, however, if it starts interfering with his work.'

'Work? I thought he was in school.'

'For summer, he's helping me. He'll be back in school in the fall.'

'What do you do, Mac? I know you own half the mountain and want it all, but what is your occupation? What is John-Michael doing to help?'

'I'm a rancher. I raise horses. He's helping out.'

'Horses? What for?' It was a long way from Kentucky and race horses.

'Rodeo horses, stock ponies, mounted police units.' He shrugged it off.

'MacKensie Horse Ranch, MHR! I've seen your brands on rodeo horses.' A smile of recognition lit her face. 'You have quite a reputation in the rodeo circuit; good stock, fair treatment.'

His eyes narrowed as he looked at her closely. 'How do you know so much about it?'

'I'm a Colorado girl. Been to many a rodeo there, and here in California, too.' She cocked her head.

'You've been around for quite a while, or was it your Dad's first?'

'Dad's first; and I hope to leave it to my son. If he doesn't get lost in foolish dreams of being a singing star.'

'And that's why you're here. To make sure he doesn't.'

'Yes. I've said I don't mind his learning, just don't fill his head with dreams and empty visions of impossible things.' He glanced around contemptuously.

Amanda felt her temper rise. How dare he sneer at her home. Were material things the only measure of a person's worth? This place suited her. When she got around to it, she would fix it up and it would be a lovely home. One he'd not be able to fault. In the meantime, if she could stand it, who was he to judge?

She was not responsible for his son. How could she help what his son thought, what he envisioned. Mac MacKensie had some nerve coming here, giving her orders on things he didn't even know about. She'd fill John-Michael's head with dreams if she wanted to.

Instantly she felt ashamed. The man was only asking her co-operation in dealing with his son, in the way he thought best for the boy. He was probably desperate to enlist her co-operation. Her temper cooled.

OK. I think you have made your point. I'll keep it in mind.'

'Then there is no need to stay longer.' He nodded and moved towards the door.

'Mac.'

He turned, raised an eyebrow.

'Could I bum a lift into town in a day or so?' She hated to ask, but did want to see if Dave had sent the banjo and pick it up when it came in. She could walk again, but it was a long way and carrying a banjo that distance would be awkward. If he were going into town anyway, perhaps he wouldn't mind giving her a ride.

'I'll be going on Thursday, late morning.'

She tilted her head. 'Thank you, I'll be ready when you are.'

'See you then.' He left.

Amanda stood still, listening to his steps on the wooden veranda, stairs, gravel. The door to the truck slammed shut and he drove away.

She moved to sink down on her cushions, still bemused by the events of the afternoon. Was Elizabeth Burke serious about having her sing at the festival on Labor Day? They were certainly casual about things in Timber. No audition, no firm contract, no percentages.

Amanda shook her head. This was not a professional show. It was a gathering of neighbours. Would they really want her there? But, why not? She was a neighbour, too, now. If it was for the community hospital, she'd be glad to donate her time. She'd talk to Dave and get his feedback. Maybe they'd do it. It would be a nice gesture for her new town. And maybe . . .

CHAPTER FIVE

THE next day Amanda spent in typical holiday fashion, lazing around, sunbathing, reading one of her new books, and panning for gold. Her skin was getting a nice tan, the colour even and golden. Her hair was turning lighter, too, with blonde streaks through it from the sun. She was looking and feeling much more relaxed, a regular schedule of sleeping and eating erasing the strains of travelling and performing.

Amanda was also writing. She finished the first song, the one she had started on her walk by the stream. A few refining touches were needed yet, but she'd wait until she was with the full band to try that, and get feedback from the others in the group. It would be easier with all of the instruments available to duplicate more closely the sound she could hear in her mind. The lyrics and melody were good, and would probably stand without much change.

She had begun another song, a couple more ideas buzzed around in her head. Pleased she was again finding composing possible, she wrote phrases and music in bits and pieces. Soon she'd put it together, see how they went together. It was a joy to write. Many of her biggest hits had been her own songs. She knew best how to write for herself; trying the melodies, searching for just the right word or phrase was challenging, something put aside in the relentless schedule of recordings and concert tours of recent years. She was pleased at the way the songs had come to her, how she could put them on paper so fast. As she relaxed, more would come, she knew it.

While not seriously planning to strike it rich,

Amanda continued to pan for gold each day. It was a soothing, restful occupation, one that permitted time for thinking or dreaming. She'd take her pan and a small glass vial and spend hours washing endless buckets of sand from the water. There were several bits and flakes in the vial. She thought they might be gold, but would have them assayed to be certain. Time enough for that at the end of the summer. For now, she was content to think it was gold; and to continue her search.

The water ran cold but, if she went during the hot part of the day, it was refreshing to splash it on herself as she toiled in the sun, sloshing, twirling, and swirling the sand and gravel from the creek bed in her black pan. Peering closely as the heavy sediment settled to the bottom. Were there more gold flakes this time? No matter, maybe in the next pan.

On Thursday morning Amanda was ready to go to town before ten. Not knowing precisely when Mac meant to go, she was ready and waiting on her veranda so as not to keep him waiting. No need to aggravate the man. He was already quick with disapproval. She wished she hadn't had to ask for his assistance, but it beat walking. Surely he wouldn't feel she was imposing if he were going down to town anyway? If he did, she knew he would have no hesitation in telling her unequivocally.

The drone of the truck became audible, gradually growing in volume, until the truck drove into view. Turning into her track, Mac stopped near the veranda.

Amanda hurried down and climbed in.

'Hi.' She smiled.

He nodded. 'Morning.' They were off.

The post office did not have any packages for Amanda Smith in general delivery, nor any mail. She was disappointed as she turned and slowly walked back out. Had Dave not yet sent it? Had the mail been delayed? Or had he sent it to the wrong town? Surely he had heard her correctly on the phone.

Still having quite a bit of time before Mac was returning, Amanda walked through the town to the only phone she was sure of. She smiled at passers by, murmuring greetings to those that spoke to her. Feeling more and more a part of Timber, she was pleased no one appeared stand-offish. In time, she would learn names and faces and really belong.

Reaching the phone booth, she dialled the familiar number. It rang and rang; no one answered. Impatiently, Amanda tapped her finger against the receiver, but still the phone rang on. Hanging up in frustration, she started back towards the truck. What a wasted trip all around.

'Get all you wanted?' Mac was waiting, sitting behind the wheel, his hat tipped forward on his forehead.

'No. None of it, in fact. I was expecting a package; nothing yet. Are you ready to go?'

'Just about. I want to pick up a few things at the grocery store. Won't be long.' He got out of the cab.

'I'll go with you. I could use a few things.' She fell into step as he walked. She had to walk fast to keep up with his longer stride. Once she almost stopped to let him go on ahead and follow at her own pace. But the distance was short, the market already in sight.

Her few things filled two bags. When Mac lifted them into the truck, he commented on them.

'Only a few things, eh? What's your heavy shopping like?'

She smiled up at him. 'I think I plan to assuage my disappointment in lots of food. Would you and John-Michael like to join me tonight for spaghetti, then hot fudge sundaes for dessert? I stocked up with plenty.'

'I think it could be arranged. Sounds good.'

Amanda carefully kept the conversation along

neutral lines as Mac drove back. They had a pleasant discussion on the various ways to cook and eat spaghetti. It was safe and would, she was sure, ensure they would not be feuding at dinner.

Mac carried one of the bags and followed Amanda into her cabin. Upon entering, Amanda, out of habit and unthinking, took off her hat, tossing it on to the dining-table as she passed. Discarding her glasses, she put them on the kitchen counter. She smiled her thanks at Mac as he put the bag on the counter.

'Good God, no wonder you wear those glasses! With those eyes, you must knock men for six!' he said involuntarily, staring down at her.

Delight and surprise flooded Amanda. She was pleased that he noticed the first time she had her glasses off. She was surprised he hadn't made more comments about wearing glasses. Then, as she saw his suddenly wooden face, the clenched jaw, she realised he had not meant to say it. With a sudden rush of understanding, protection almost, Amanda realised Mac wished he were anywhere in the world but where he was. Such a compliment was totally foreign to him.

Gently, in hopes of easing the situation, Amanda teased him. 'Sorry, Mac, compliments won't get you anywhere. This place is mine and will remain so.' She was pleased to see him relax a little.

'Can't blame a man for trying,' he said. 'I'm off now. John-Michael and I will see you later, then.'

'Come about six. You can both help me with salad and garlic bread.'

'I'll bring some wine. It'll round off the meal.'

'Good, I look forward to it. What's that?'

An engine could be heard, gravel spinning on the driveway. Moving to the window, Amanda gave a brief exclamation of surprise then, with a lightened heart, dashed out to greet the new arrival, scarcely aware that Mac had followed her to the front window.

'Dave, oh, Dave!' She flew to meet the bearded man climbing off the big Harley motorcycle. Swept off her feet by his embrace, she was spun round and round. He gave her a big kiss, setting her down, loosening his hold on her, but keeping his hands locked behind her back, hers around his neck.

'Hello, Mandy, sweet. Glad to see me?' he said, with a sweet smile. His hair was the same rich brown as his beard, worn long, brushing his shoulders, kept from his eyes with an old bandana tied like a sweatband. His shirt was faded, partially covered by an old, worn, leather waistcoat. Faded jeans and scuffy boots completed his attire.

'I sure am. What are you doing here? How did you *find* me? Oh, it is good to see you. I've missed you. Vacations are fun, but I have missed everyone. How is everybody?' She smiled in complete happiness, giving him a hug.

'What do I answer first? I've come to bring you your blasted banjo, and to see what you are up to.' He looked up and swept his eyes around. 'Oh, oh. Who's the dude on the porch? Is he mad at you, or me?'

Amanda turned to find Mac's glare on her. Gingerly she disengaged herself from Dave's embrace, a sinking in the pit of her stomach. Just when she thought she was getting somewhere with her neighbour, he had to see this. No telling what conclusions he was jumping to.

She glanced quickly at Dave and winced just a little. If she ever wanted to convince Mac they were hippies, now was the time. Dave had patches on his denims, old western shirt, and a stained bandana. He looked totally disreputable. No matter that he was a wealthy member of her troupe, responsible and respected in the music industry, or that he was from a good family in Colorado. Mac would think the worst. She turned

back. So much for her incognito summer. She'd have
to explain.

Mac descended the steps and moved to his truck,
his face set with stern disapproval.

'Mac,' she called bravely. 'I'd like you to meet
Dave. This is a neighbour of mine, Dave, Mac
MacKensie. He just gave me a lift to town.' She
trailed off as Mac disdainfully regarded the two of
them briefly before climbing into his truck.

She moved quickly to the window. 'Please, Mac,
won't you stay? I can explain.'

'I think not. You'll understand why we won't join
you for dinner, too. Though I'm sure you'll not miss
our company tonight.'

'But the spaghetti . . .'

'So long, Miss Smith.' He slammed the truck into
gear and jerked back.

'What's all that about?' Dave asked, joining her as
the grey pick-up made the turn up the driveway.

She sighed and turned, linking her arm with his.
'Nothing. Just an impossible man . . . that I wish I
knew better.'

She smiled at Dave. 'Tell me about Evie and
everything. Did you really come to bring the banjo, and
check up on me? And from where? You didn't
drive all the way from L.A. on that bike?'

'No, of course not. It's Marc's. I picked it up at his
place in San Francisco. That's bad enough. Almost
three hours it took me. And, yes, I came to check up
on you, and I brought the banjo, and messages from
the gang. How's the vacation? Looks like it is doing
you good. You look terrific.'

'It is. Oh, Dave, come and see my house,' she
invited proudly. 'It's going to be nice, I think, though
there's loads to do yet. But I'm in no hurry. I like the
planning and changing. And I've written a couple of
songs, as I told you on the phone. I want your

opinion, of course. But I think they are good. I may write a dozen before the summer is over. Come on in. This is my living room.'

Amanda proudly showed off her place, ending her tour in the kitchen, and chatting with Dave while she put away the groceries, anxious for the messages he relayed from the others in the band, and his wife, Evie. They discussed their forthcoming trip to Nashville, plans to meet in San Francisco, to fly east together.

Finally Amanda played the new songs for him. He listened without comment, without expression. Only when she had finished the last notes of the second song did he speak enthusiastically.

'They are good, sweetheart! That first one should go to the top. They are like some of your earlier ones and *Sing the Mountain Down*, yet different enough not to be repetitions of other songs. I think they will be great. If vacations do that for you, take two or three a year.'

'I'm so glad you liked it, cousin. I thought they were pretty good, but I can't always tell. I knew you'd tell me true.'

'Yes. Of course I will. We don't want any clunkers. Got any more songs?'

'In my head. I'll have another before Nashville probably.' She put the guitar aside. 'OK. You've given me the messages from everyone else, now tell me how you and Evie are doing. How's the baby? Everything OK?'

Evie was Dave's wife, pregnant with their first child. Amanda and Dave, first cousins, had been best friends since childhood. He had been with her the entire time she had been singing; making road arrangements, leading the band, protecting his cousin. Evie had been a devoted fan who had asked for an autograph when they had played in Dallas a couple of years ago. She began dating Dave, then married him. Amanda was very fond of her and pleased for Dave in his happiness. The expected child was looked forward to eagerly by the whole troupe. Amanda hoped the arrival of the baby might cause Dave to want to travel less, as she herself was ready to settle a little bit. Fewer weeks on the road would suit her fine. Especially since she had her own place now to care for, to work on.

They talked fast and furiously, catching up on all the news as if they had been parted months, instead of weeks. Making plans for the autumn tour, future road deals. Amanda cooked the spaghetti, with only a small pang of regret that Mac and John-Michael would not be there to share it with her. She and Dave ate; but there was no wine.

Dave stayed the night, slept on the narrow bed in the second bedroom. His view was different from Mandy's, so he duly admired the scene from her bedroom window the next morning before leaving early for his return journey. He smiled indulgently at his cousin's enthusiasm for the bluebells on the hill. A flower was a flower to him.

'I'm so glad you came,' Amanda said, hugging him goodbye. 'I'll see you in a couple of weeks in San Francisco.'

'OK. Take care of yourself. Hey, Mandy.' He tilted her chin up gently. 'Don't go falling for that bad-tempered neighbour of yours, you hear?'

She flushed a little. 'I'm not.'

He frowned. 'Not convincing. If you do, I'll talk to him. He'd better do you right.'

'Yes, Papa,' she replied saucily.

He smacked her bottom. 'You behave.' A quick kiss, a wave and with a roar the motorcycle came to life and off he spun. Amanda waved goodbye until he was out of sight. She was so very fond of her cousin Dave.

She felt a little lost when he first left, pottering around for a while, nothing holding her attention. Finally, she grabbed her pan and headed for the creek. The great gold discovery just might be today! How Dave had laughed last night when she told him of her panning activity. She didn't care. She found it soothing and relaxing and she loved it.

Soon, lost in the concentration of panning, she swirled the water, flushing out the sand and grit, the gurgling of the stream a pleasant melody, blocking out cares and worries. Its soothing rhythm was soporific to her. She lost track of time.

A shadow on the water caused her to look up. Startled, she found herself gazing into the glittering eyes of Mac MacKensic. Nearby, tethered to a tree, was the lovely bay gelding he rode. She was surprised; she had not heard their approach.

'Good morning,' she said, standing. Oh, her knees were stiff, her back sore.

'What are you doing?'

'Panning for gold.' What did it look like, she wondered.

'Is that how you plan to make your living here?'

'No.'

He waited a moment, but when she added nothing to that, he spoke again. 'Did your *friend* leave?'

'Yes.' Should she try to explain now that Dave was her cousin?

'This morning?' Mac ground out as if goaded.

'Yes, this morning. We missed you last night,' she taunted, 'the spaghetti was delicious.'

'Dessert, too, I imagine.'

She looked puzzled. They had not had dessert; Dave didn't especially like ice cream. As she looked at Mac, a small flicker of fear ran through her when he stepped on the rocks, advancing deliberately towards her, carelessly disregarding the water splashing on his boots. Coming right up to her. Crowding her on her rock.

'Sorry I missed it last night. I'll have my share now.' He reached out and caught her arms, pulling her ruthlessly up against him, finding her mouth with his, kissing her harshly, his strong lips forcing hers against her teeth. A punishing display of male physical strength.

After only a moment of shocked paralysis, Amanda struggled to pull free, pushing against him, twisting, kicking, but to no avail. His fingers bit hard into her arms, his head forcing hers back until she thought her neck would break. Finally, eons later, he released her.

'I should have come last night,' he said provocatively, anger evident on his face.

'In a pig's eye,' she spat, jerking away from him. The movement caught her off balance and, with an involuntary shriek, she fell backwards into the creek. The icy water knocked the breath from her. While the creek was not deep, it was sufficiently so to cushion her from the sharp rocks, to soak her thoroughly with the icy liquid, swirling and splashing around her. She sat up, shaking water from the eyes.

'Next time be more generous with your favours,' Mac said.

'No favours,' she gritted, sitting in the cold water as it raced around her. 'Dave is my cousin.'

'And I'm your Uncle Fred,' he retorted.

Amanda looked up in surprise, a small gurgle of laughter escaping as she struggled to stand against the stream's pull. 'I don't have an Uncle Fred.'

'Maybe you should. Here.' Mac held out a strong hand, helping her back on to the flat rock. Water was streaming from her.

'Mac,' she said sweetly, opening her eyes wide and coming closer. Her shirt and shorts dripped water, droplets glistening on her arms and legs. 'Next time you kiss someone, use a little more gentleness.' She moved up to him, offering her lips, swaying towards him.

He took her gently, lowering his lips against hers again. Amanda moved quickly into his arms, encircling his neck with her wet hands, pressing herself against the length of him, feeling him shrink back from her dripping clothes. She moved in closer. Let him share the icy water. She was freezing!

As his lips moved persuasively against hers, she forgot the revenge she had tried. Forgot all else save the feel of his mouth against hers, moving gently now. Now exciting. His mouth warm and firm, moving against hers. She gave herself up to the enjoyment of the embrace.

'You are a brat,' Mac said against her lips after a long moment.

'Mm.' She did not want to loosen contact.

'I'm all wet.'

Another gurgle of laughter bubbled up, escaped. She was thrust unceremoniously back, still laughing. Mac's shirt and jeans were both wet where she had pressed against him. She laughed at the sight, pleased to see she had got him a little wet, too. Next time, maybe he wouldn't be so quick to think he could get away with anything.

His eyes narrowed dangerously, taking in her pleased expression. He glanced arrogantly down the length of her, at the damp cloth moulding her figure like a second skin, raising his eyes to meet hers.

'On second thoughts, maybe I should forget about the property and take you instead.' He drew a finger insolently along the neckline of her shirt, trailing it down to the V of her breasts.

Angrily she knocked his hand away.

'You arrogant swine.'

'Oh, I don't know,' he said easily. 'You felt pretty compliant a minute ago.'

Amanda's eyes raked him as they stood there, taking in the casual, arrogant stance of the man, the outline of her own body still visible in the damp of his shirt.

'See? Visible evidence,' he mocked as her eyes traced the damp spots.

'You . . . You arrogant . . .' she sputtered for words, 'cowboy pig!'

He roared with laughter at her effort, infuriating Amanda.

In an instant, almost without thought, she stooped, swept up a load of water in her pan and threw it full in his face, soaking him with the icy spray.

'Maybe that'll wash the thought from your mind,' she said from between clenched teeth.

The ominous, angry look in his eye made her step back, eyeing the stream bed for a means of escape, or a weapon. A rock?

'Vixen. I wouldn't pick one up, if I were you, unless you were sure you would use it,' he threatened, aware of her intent.

'I'd be sure,' she lied. Holding the pan before her as if warding off a sword, she glanced quickly around. 'I believe you are on my property, Mr MacKensie. Would you be kind enough to leave.' Sarcastic words which she hoped would veil her own uncertainty.

Amanda did not run into individuals like this in the entertainment field. An occasional drunk trying to be too amorous; an over-enthusiastic fan; but something Amanda could deal with. Here she was decidedly at a disadvantage.

He held her eyes as he answered. 'Point taken, Miss Smith. Though I would mention to you that people up here are more polite. It is usually perfectly acceptable to cross someone's land, as long as no harm is done.'

No harm done! Amanda wondered when she could fully assess all the damage.

He turned and easily negotiated the stream bed, leisurely moving to his horse. Amanda pointedly ignored him, gathering her things to head for home to dry off. What gall! Just because she had had a male for dinner last night, and a cousin to boot, did not give Mac any right to her favours, as he said. Arrogant beast!

She stormed home as he rode in the opposite direction, but Amanda couldn't erase the memory of Mac's embrace as easily as she should have. Taking a hot shower to warm up, she found herself dwelling on the second kiss, the sweetness of his lips against hers, of his arms holding her close. Her heart skipped a beat. What had started as revenge for his first savage assault, had turned out to be something she had wished would go on and on. Would the opportunity ever arise again? Did she want it to?

CHAPTER SIX

AMANDA did not pan for gold for the next two days. She stayed close to her house, as if the walls themselves would hide her and protect her against further onslaughts from the opposition. More than once, however, she found herself lost in a daydream involving herself and Mac, ending with another kiss. They were harmless fantasies, she told herself, a purely physical reaction, and dreaming about them would probably get them out of her system. Probably.

Music resounded from her fingers as she picked out complex songs for the guitar. New words and melodies crowded her mind and she set them down for further work. She was glad for the time to lose herself in her music, for the time devoted strictly to the discipline and the challenge. The pages of words and notes grew as she experimented with different phrases, different melodies, keeping the ones she liked, throwing out anything that didn't sound as good on the second day.

She was relaxed, content to enjoy her lazy days, the quiet, slow pace of life, only vaguely conscious of a nagging feeling, of something missing.

The afternoon was warm and still when Amanda tipped back in her chair and reached for her guitar again. Idly she picked out the tune echoing in her head. She ought to write it down. It could be another big hit. But she hesitated. It was not clearly defined, yet, she told herself. And if the words were what she felt, she was not ready for the world to know it. She wasn't sure she knew it. Besides, as often as she had heard the words in her head the last few days, and played it, she doubted she'd ever forget. She'd wait a while before writing it down. No rush. It was too frail to stand up alone, too precious to be exposed to the critical attention of another listener.

Soon, maybe. For now, it was only for her.

'La la la-la-la, umm, mmm,' she hummed, putting words to the melody. Playing it over and over, never tiring of the repetition, pausing only a moment before beginning yet again.

During one of the pauses, the soft clop clop of a horse's walk penetrated her absorption. From the sound of it, Mac was riding this way. She smiled with anticipation, sat a little straighter in her chair. Briefly she wished she had brushed her hair out. It did look better flowing than tied back. Too late now.

How to play this meeting? Icy indignation? Cool unconcern, or tepid friendship? One thing, Amanda did not believe she could pretend nothing had happened. That the kisses at the creek had never been.

She was surprised at the disappointment that flooded through her when John-Michael rode into view. It was not Mac after all, but his son, riding his sleek chestnut. His legs dangled down, a guitar slung across his back. With a small sigh, Amanda forced her face into a smile and waved. No reason to take her disappointment out on John-Michael.

'Hi,' he called as he approached. 'Got time for a lesson?'

'Sure do.' Bless his heart, he asked for little, and took such great delight in the lessons she gave. She felt better.

He slid off the horse, tethered it to the bottom post of the stair railing, and climbed the steps.

'Your horse? I've seen it before,' Amanda asked, nodding to the chestnut nibbling at the grass near the cabin.

'One of ours. Dad raises horses, you know, so we

always have them around.' He drew one of the chairs closer to Amanda.

'Been practising much?' she asked as he settled in.

'Not as much as I'd like,' John-Michael replied, strumming a little. 'My old man's been on my case the last couple of days. "Do this, do that. Is such-and-such taken care of?" Jeez, it's enough to drive you crazy. He's set against the guitar, too. He didn't seem to mind so much when I started, but now it's "You'll never make a living with that. If you'd spend as much time on your school work as you do on that damn fool guitar, you'd do better." Gosh, Mandy, school's not even in session!'

She smiled. 'Did you tell him that?'

'Yes. He blew up.' John-Michael stared off into space as if reliving the incident. He shifted in his chair and looked at Amanda. 'I don't care, though. It's not hurting anyone if I learn to play.' John-Michael shrugged. 'He doesn't like me much anyway.'

'Oh, John-Michael, I'm sure that is not true.' Amanda was quick to respond to defend Mac. 'Sometimes parents and teenagers don't get along so well for a time, but it's not for lack of love, just want of a little understanding. I know you have heard of the generation gap. Some of it is based on fact. Different generations look at things differently. It is a function of the time in which you do your growing up.'

'I don't know. He's been especially awful the last couple of days.'

Amanda wondered if the incident at the creek had anything to do with intensifying Mac's anti-guitar stance. Mac had asked her to refrain from leading John-Michael on with foolish dreams, but had not forbidden lessons. Why be so down on the boy at home? She watched the pleasure on John-Michael's face as he struggled to master the music. He liked it. It wasn't hurting anyone, and she would continue the lessons unless specifically requested to desist by Mac.

'It sounds good,' Amanda said a few minutes later. 'Ready for some more chords now? Get these under control and we'll start picking and developing a good backlog of songs you can play.'

'Good. I'll like that. Were you playing when I got here?' he asked, eyeing the papers on the table.

'Not exactly. Jotting down some music. I write a little,' she replied modestly.

'No kidding? How do you think up the tunes?'

She shrugged. 'I just hear them in my head and write what I hear. Do you want to write?'

'Naw. I just want to play for fun. Dad's all worried I'll run off and try to make it big as a singer.' He shook his head again.

'You don't want to try?'

'No, I want to be a rancher like Dad. I don't know if I can, though. He gets annoyed with me so much. I try to do what he wants, but I seem to get to him. I don't know. But the music business would be too hard, I think. Too much competition, cut-throat dealings. A lot of travelling.'

'It has its rewards,' she said gently. 'But I think you're wise to stick to something you know you will like and can be good at doing.'

'I guess. OK, show me the new chords.'

Amanda enjoyed the time she spent with John-Michael, in spite of her initial disappointment. He was bright, pleasant and enthusiastic. Eager to learn all she could teach him, he was attentive and quick to pick up on all the pointers she gave. They tried several different songs, Amanda playing along slowly with John-Michael. They sang together loudly and with a lot of gusto until John-Michael stopped during one song, watching and listening to Amanda as she finished.

'You are *good*,' he said when she paused, still strumming her guitar.

Abruptly she stopped. Had he made any connection? She did so want to remain plain Mandy Smith. She forced a smile, laying down the instrument. 'Thanks. I got the banjo. Want to see it?' Not waiting for a reply, she jumped up and went inside to get it. Of all the people to guard against, the one person in Timber she *knew* listened to her records, had albums in his home. She had better watch herself, or blow her cover.

As she grabbed her banjo, she wondered if the knowledge of who she was would affect the friendship she and John-Michael were building. Maybe she was making too much of this identity business. Still, it was hard to break old ideas. For the last few years, the only people she really felt comfortable with, felt were her true friends, were the few she had known before she had made it big. Before 'Amanda' was a nationally known name. She'd hold off on any revelations for a while.

John-Michael was still playing the new chords when she went back to the veranda. He glanced up and smiled uncertainly, watching her closely as she sat down.

'You want to try it?' she offered.

'No, maybe later. Play something.'

'OK, how about *Oh, Susannah?*'

'Good.'

As Amanda played the familiar tune, John-Michael's face brightened. He softly slapped his hand against his knee in time with the music. From that favourite to others, Amanda played one after the other. Humming along, but not singing. Finally, after a medley of Stephen Foster songs, she lay back in her chair, flexing her fingers.

'Whew, I haven't done that much in an long time.'

'You are great! How long have you been playing? You ought to try it professionally.'

She smiled. 'I've been playing since I was a kid, younger than you. My cousins and I were always trying to outdo each other. These steel strings can hurt after a while. You want to try now?'

'Yes, though just to fool around with.' John-Michael took it and tried out a few tentative strokes, trying the chords, different strumming rhythms. Looking up to Amanda, he said, 'You're right, my fingers hurt already. Thanks. When I get better, I want to expand to this, too. I like guitar better, though.'

'Me, too. Want some lemonade?'

'I've got to be going. Thank you for the lesson.' He stood up, a tall, lanky boy. Before many years, he'd fill out and become a man in similar stature to his father. Amanda felt a small pang. Would she know him then? She rose with him and walked him to the top of the steps.

'It's a lovely horse,' she admired.

'Yes. Thanks. He's the one I ride the most. I like him too. He's only seven. Born on the ranch. I've raised and trained him myself.'

'Looks as if you've done a good job. Do you raise anything besides horses? Any cattle?'

Amanda was still rather surprised they had a working ranch. The majority of the land she had seen was so wooded she didn't think it would provide enough pasture for horses. They required so much more pasture than cattle. Still, she remembered the rolling, grassy hill falling away from Mac's hilltop home. Maybe there were hidden acres of open pasture that she had not seen.

'No, we raise just the horses, except for the few head of cattle for our own use. We sell the horses to rodeos and mounted police.'

'Umm.' She nodded her head. The ranch in Colorado where she had grown up was primarily a cattle enterprise. The land was different, too, from this California mountain area. She'd like to see over MacKensie's Horse Ranch one day. See the differences in the operations.

'Thanks again for the lesson. I'll be back.' John-Michael slung his guitar over his back and swung himself lithely up on his horse. Tugging gently on the bridle, he turned and ambled off towards home.

Amanda watched him leave, then turned slowly back to her music. Two MacKensies in one day would be too much to expect. Slowly she started on her song again.

The next day Amanda dressed in shorts and a sleeveless, loose top. Just because she had had a run in with Mr MacKensie a few days ago, she was no longer going to be put off in her pursuit of fun. She liked panning for gold. The time spent out of doors was a welcome change from recording studios, aeroplanes and hotel rooms. She wanted to spend as much time in the fresh air as she could while she had the opportunity. The weather was glorious, her duties minimal while on holiday. She would not let the experience of her last outing affect her going again. Today she'd pan for gold.

She grabbed her hat and the gold pan and was off. While it was warm in the sun, there were several high, puffy white clouds dotting the blue expanse. A slight breeze skipped across the grass; the air in the shade a few degrees cooler than previous days. A cooling trend coming in, she thought.

Going directly to her usual spot, Amanda began the now familiar task.

Time slid by. Unaware of passing minutes, Amanda contentedly washed gravel and grit patiently with pan after pan of water. Twice she thought she spotted gold flecks, carefully claiming them from the pan bottom and placing them in the small vial she carried.

One of the harmless clouds drifted before the sun, shading the patch of earth Amanda was working on. Immediately, she felt cooler. The mountain air itself was not warm; the sun gave the day the warmth she had been enjoying. In the shade, the water also grew colder, turned dark grey.

Glancing up, Amanda was reassured. It was a brief interlude; already the cloud was moving on, releasing the sun to resume its warming functions.

A short time later Amanda stood up, stretching. Her back ached a little, her hands were cold. She leaped to the shore, wandering a few feet upstream to an area fairly free of rocks. She sat down, stretching her legs out before her, leaning back to soak up the sun's rays. She took off her hat, using it as a pillow, lay back down. The sun was hot on her face, her arms, her legs. Slowly she relaxed, easing the tight muscles across her shoulders, easing away tension. The creek played a gentle music. Amanda dozed.

A shadow covered her face, blocking the sun's warmth again. She frowned a little. If the cloud blocked all of the sun, she'd start to get cold. Squinting, she looked up to judge how large this cloud was, startled to find herself gazing into Mac's amused face.

'Taking a sun bath?' he asked politely, his eyes taking in her recumbent figure.

She shook her head, scrambling to sit up, feeling decidedly at a disadvantage as he squatted down beside her. She put her hat back on, noticing Mac's horse tethered to a nearby shrub.

'I didn't hear you come up,' she said, scooting back a little, away from his overwhelming nearness. This was twice she had missed his approach. Maybe being by the creek wasn't all to the good.

'I think you might have been asleep,' he said gravely.

She nodded. 'I was, I guess. I've been panning and was a little stiff, so I lay down. The heat put me out.'

'Any luck?'

'Only flakes. But I don't care. I love it. I don't really expect to strike it rich.'

'Still a lot of gold in these hills. The mines around Timber produced over two million dollars worth of gold in their prime. It is estimated the Mother Lode has more than two hundred million dollars still buried in the hills.'

'Around here?'

'Here to Placerville, and north. You're panning for placer gold; lode gold can be found around here too, but not as easily.'

'Lode gold? I thought gold was gold.'

'Placer gold is loose, gold that's been worked up and out by nature, tumbling free in the streams and rivers of the Mother Lode during flood season. Settling out sometimes miles from the vein that produced it. Lode gold is the gold still in veins. In this area, quartz is usually found with gold. If you find quartz, examine it carefully to see if there are gold traces. Come on, I'll show you.'

Mac rose to his full height. Amanda slowly stood up, a little at a loss for his change of attitude. It had been daggers at dawn before; now, almost friendly overtures. Warily she followed as he headed briskly upstream, his eyes on the creek bed. There was no awkwardness, no time to think about how to react to the man. He appeared to be ignoring their last confrontation. Far be it from Amanda to drag it up. She hurried to keep up with him.

'OK. Here.' He stopped and waited for her to catch up. With long strides, he left the bank, stepping nimbly on to the large rocks and boulders rising up through the rambling water. Pausing on a large, sloping boulder, he reached into the clear liquid on the lee side of the rock. He drew out two white, translucent stones, discoloured along one side.

'See here,' he pointed along a crack in one rock. 'This is quartz, lots of it around here. These veins on the rock are similar to the ones found with gold.'

Amanda peered at the rock, taking it from him to examine.

'See the rust colouring on the side?'

She nodded, conscious of his hands pointing out the traces on the rock, conscious of his shoulder close to her own as he bent to point out the markings on the rock. Concentrate on what he is telling me, she admonished herself.

'It is from the pyrite, fool's gold. It's often present where gold is found.'

Amanda looked around the creek, stooping to scoop up a few other white stones, discarding one immediately when she saw it was a smooth pebble, not the ragged, translucent stone she was looking for. The others she examined more closely. Here and there were black lines which cut into the rocks.

'Sometimes you can crack the rock open, finding the gold on the outside has been worn away, but a bit of the vein inside still has some of the ore.'

'Will it be shiny?' She tossed back the rocks, picked up new ones.

'You'll know it's gold, it looks the same in sun or shade. Not polished like jewellery, but definitely gold.'

She nodded, examining the rocks, tossing them away when they did not have what she wanted. Mac also pulled rocks from the stream bed, returning them to the water more quickly than Amanda. Silently they dug up white stones, looking them over, threw them back. Twice Amanda hesitated, then put the stones in her pan for later study.

She lost track of the time when Mac turned to her, hand outstretched to her.

'Here you are, traces of gold.'

She took the rock, white on the one side. Turning it over, she saw a wide band of grey-black mixed with a dull metal. Just traces, but he was right, she did know it was gold. She raised shining eyes to him.

'It's gold!' She held it out for him to take back.

'It's for you. You can keep it.'

'But you found it. I can't take it.'

He smiled. 'Plenty more where it came from. I told you, two hundred million dollars worth.' He flicked the rock, still in her outstretched hand. 'This is probably worth less than fifty cents if you scraped it off the rock.'

'It's still gold,' she defended happily, looking again at the traces on the side of the stone. All the flakes and grains of gold painstakingly panned from the creek over the last few weeks did not equal the amount of ore displayed on this hunk of quartz.

'Yes,' he said, 'it is gold.'

She looked closely at the surrounding land. 'Does it come from here, the quartz?' Maybe they could find the vein, the lode gold.

'Probably not. In the spring, when the snow melts from the higher elevations, this old creek swells considerably. It's a raging river then, moving a tremendous amount of material with it: rocks, stones, logs, debris. Over the years it has washed the stones down from higher elevations, who knows how far. In the late fall, the water is so low it's only a small trickle, scarcely moving at all.'

Amanda looked at the water. 'It's hard to believe,' she murmured. Where would she be in late autumn, in October? On tour somewhere? Cutting a new album? No matter, she'd be sure to have a few days here. This was her home now and she wanted to see it in all its different guises.

'Are we below the snowline here?' she asked, trying to envisage snow on the trees, piled on the boulders.

Mac stared at her for a moment. 'Didn't you ask about that before buying?'

She shook her head.

'Depends on the winter. Usually get a few storms through that dump on us. If it's a mild winter, then no.' He moved back to the bank. 'I've got things to do. You keep on with your search, if you like.'

'No, I'm hungry. I'll stop for today.' Tightly clutching her precious rock, she gained the bank, turning for another look at the spot so she'd recognise it when she came again. As they started back, she looked around again, puzzled.

'Mac, is this my land?'

'No, your property ends a few yards from where you were napping.'

'Then I can't come tomorrow.' Disappointment coursed through her, was evident in her voice.

'As long as you don't set up dredging operations, you can search for gold anywhere on the creek,' he replied.

Amanda considered this, further puzzled. She glanced at him from under the brim on her hat as he moved casually along. Was this the same man she had met before? The one so adamant to get rid of her, to regain the propery he coveted? This the same man who considered her a hippie, a jobless freeloader who should go out and look for work? Whatever had wrought such a change?

Suddenly Amanda recalled their meeting before Dave had come. Mac had said perhaps he could accomplish his goal with kindness. Was he trying that tack? Being kind to her, becoming a friend in hopes of talking her into letting him have the property?

They reached his horse, dozing in the sun. Mac untethered him, turning back to Amanda. He regarded

her for a long moment, looking at her mouth,
reminding her vividly of their last meeting by the
creek, of the harsh kiss; and the one filled with delight.
Nervously she licked her lips. Would he kiss her
again?

'Look for your treasure, Mandy. What you find you
may keep. No strings.'

She was startled at his largess. Had she misjudged
the man? 'Thank you. I'll ... I'll let you know if I
find the big strike.'

'You do that.'

As he rode away, Amanda felt a small loss. Slowly
she headed homeward, her spirits rising a little as she
realised she and Mac had spent well over an hour
together with no altercations. She examined her rock,
rubbing gently against the gold embedded on the
stone. He had found it and given it to her. It might not
be worth much, as he had said, but she'd never know
because she didn't plan to take it anywhere to be
valued. It was worth a great deal to her just as it was.

She dwelt on the pleasant companionship shared as
they both had searched for gold in the cold waters of
the creek. Whenever she looked at her 'golden rock' in
the future, she'd remember the pleasure of the day.

CHAPTER SEVEN

SHOPPING was becoming a minor irritation. As Amanda prepared another list of things she wanted, she pondered on how she was going to get to town and, more importantly, how she'd get back with the groceries she was picking up. She'd have to give serious thought to obtaining some type of vehicle for transportation. She could not depend on the constant largess of others for her transportation needs. The lack of taxi service made having a car almost a necessity here. She'd look into it further when she returned from Nashville. Dave would give her some advice, she was sure. In the meantime, she frowned, she still had to get to town today.

A horn sounded in the front. Amanda crossed to the window to peer out. Mac's big grey truck was in her yard, John-Michael at the wheel. He blew the horn again.

Amanda opened her door. 'Hi,' she called. 'What are you up to?'

'Hi. Dad's let me take the truck into town to get a few supplies. Want anything?'

'I sure do. In fact, I could use a lift. Is that OK?'

'Sure, come on.'

'I didn't know you drove,' Amanda said a few minutes later as she climbed in and John-Michael carefully negotiated the turn from the driveway to the highway. She was surprised he was old enough, but she wasn't particularly good at judging people's ages.

'Just got my licence a couple of months ago,' he said proudly. 'Dad doesn't let me go too often myself yet, but he's too busy today and we need some antiseptic ointment for one of the horses. Got scratched on something.'

'Well, you're a lifesaver for me. I need a few groceries,' Amanda replied, settling back in the seat. 'Are you in a hurry? I won't be long.'

'No hurry,' he said, concentrating on the road.

Amanda remained silent as they negotiated the turns down the highway to Timber. A new driver did not need distracting passengers, so she turned her attention to the scenery, familiar now, as it flashed by.

Joining John-Michael at the truck after her shopping was finished, Amanda asked if she had time enough to make a call.

'Sure. Don't you have a phone at home?'

'No, and when I get back, I plan to remedy that. The phone company said they could instal one by then.' It was another minor inconvenience of living up here.

'Get back? Mandy, you're not leaving?'

'Yes, but just for a short trip. That's why I need to make the phone call today, to confirm travel arrangements. There's a phone at the bus depot.'

'Yes, I know. One in Murphy's too.' John-Michael started the truck, pulling carefully out on to the main street.

'How long will you be gone?'

'Only a week or so. John-Michael, would you be able to give me a lift to the bus depot when I leave?'

'I'd be glad to, Mandy. Just let me know when.'

'You sure it would be all right with your father?'

'I don't see why he'd mind. I'll wait for you here.' He stopped the truck near the phone.

Amanda was relieved to talk with Evie, Dave's wife, rather than her cousin. Evie did not keep her on the phone long, only verifying travel plans and noting when Amanda would be joining the group. They were meeting in San Fancisco, flying from there to Nashville.

'I'm all set,' Amanda announced, rejoining John-Michael. 'Thanks for waiting.'

'That's OK.' They began the homeward journey. 'When do you go?'

'Next Tuesday. Will that be a convenient day?'

'Sure.'

'I'll be back Thursday week, if I can get a lift back too.'

'Sure.'

John-Michael did not talk the remainder of the trip back. Amanda watched the pines and madrones pass in a steady stream as they climbed towards her cabin, a feeling of gladness, of well-being and happiness expanding within her. She loved this area. The tall Ponderosa pines, the leafy madrone and dogwood, the fragrant cedar, low-lying mountain misery, the curvy, hilly, narrow roads. How glad she was she had stopped here, had found a small niche in Timber.

'I'll help you carry in your bags,' John-Michael said as he stopped the engine.

'Thank you, sir.' She smiled at him, struck again by his resemblance to his father. *Déjà vu.* A tall man helping her unload her groceries. That time marred by the unexpected and unexplained arrival of her cousin; by Mac's uncompromising view of the circumstances. Oddly, she had never explained it to him. Was he still believing the worst of that visit? Amanda wished she had explained, wished the opportunity to do so would come.

'John-Michael, would you and your father care to join me for dinner tonight? I have spaghetti, and owe your Dad a spaghetti dinner. We had planned to have one and then he declined. I have plenty for all of us.'

'Gee, I don't know. We hardly ever go out, except

to Aunt Elizabeth's. I'll ask him, Mandy. But I don't know.'

'Well, if he can't come, maybe you could,' she suggested. 'I'd like to have you.'

'I'd like it too, I love spaghetti,' he replied enthusiastically. 'What time?'

'Six-ish. Bring your guitar and we'll play.'

'Great! I'll see you then.'

Promptly at six, Amanda heard the truck turn into the track. She had changed into clean brushed denim jeans and a soft blue top which threw her large eyes into prominence. She had considered leaving her hair loose, but decided against it. Opening the door, she was warmed as she saw Mac climbing from the driver's seat. He had come. Behind him, John-Michael followed, carrying his guitar.

'Hallo,' she called gaily, a warm smile of welcome on her face.

'Hallo.' Mac's face was grave, but Amanda was not put off. She knew he rarely smiled. John-Michael was looking happy.

'Red wine.' Mac offered a small bag to Amanda. 'I remember I was to supply that.'

So he had remembered their other dinner arrangement too. Did he also regret their plans had not materialised that evening?

'Can we help you do anything?' John-Michael asked, following Amanda into the kitchen.

'Sure, want to spread the garlic butter on the sourdough bread? We'll heat it and be ready to eat.'

A pot of spaghetti sauce bubbled lazily on a back burner, the aroma rising from it tantalising their appetites as they all crowded into the small kitchen. A larger pot of boiling water cooked spaghetti.

Mac took off his hat and placed it on an empty, out of the way spot on the counter. His burnished copper hair shone in the later afternoon light, thick and wavy, almost curls where it grew a little longer on his neck. His mahogany tan was a dramatic contrast. Amanda knew she was staring, blushed when his eyes met, held hers. He was so very attractive. It was with a real effort that she forced her gaze away, forced herself to remember her other guest, and get John-Michael started on the bread.

'I was surprised Dad came,' John-Michael confessed in a low voice. 'I asked him when I got home and he said yes right away.'

'Well, I'm glad you both could come. I'm not much of a cook, don't do much of it, but I can make spaghetti.'

'How do you manage if you don't cook? I thought all women cooked,' John-Michael said.

Mac spoke up, the low voice of his son carrying, 'I thought so, too. You can't? And you invite innocent people over to eat?' Was that a small twinkle in his eye? Amanda felt as if she were again confronting a stranger, not the neighbour she had known for the last few weeks.

'I can manage *this* dinner,' she replied, 'but in Los Angeles I eat out a lot, or with friends,' she said vaguely.

'Is that where you lived before you came here?' John-Michael asked, handing her the loaf, wrapped in foil, ready for the oven.

'Yes.'

'Why did you leave?'

'Aside from the aspect of buying this place simply to annoy me,' Mac put in smoothly, crossing his arms and leaning against the sink. A man with every evidence of enjoying himself.

She threw him a saucy look, her eyes sparkling, 'That was just an added stroke of luck. I had no idea when I bought this property that annoying you would be a part of it.'

'Speaking of which, I have a proposition to make to you about this place.'

'Oh, no.' Amanda looked at him, her lips tightening. Surely he wasn't going to ask her to leave yet again? She opened her mouth to tell him she did not plan to sell, but he raised his hand, continuing.

'No, hear me out. I want to buy an option on this place. If and when you ever do sell it, you will agree to give me first crack at it. At the fair market value, of course. That way, even if you're eighty-three before you are ready to leave, I will know I can have the property back eventually.'

She smiled at that.

He did, too, briefly. 'I know, if you wait until you are eighty-three, I'd be a hundred-and-three, and probably not here any more, but you know what I mean.'

She nodded. 'I doubt you are that much older than I am, Mac. You look to be much younger than fifty,' she said drily.

He was startled. 'I'm thirty-eight, how old are you?'

'Twenty-eight.'

'My compliments, you carry your years well.' He inclined his head, narrowing his eyes as he studied her.

'Thank you.'

She paused, forgetting the by-play, thinking. From her point of view, she saw no reason not to take him up on his offer, though if she continued on the way she had been going, she'd live in Timber the rest of her life. Of course, she'd travel as part of her job, as long as the popularity lasted. But she would always be able to come home between tours and recording treks. If she could further develop her writing skills, eventually she would reduce personal appearances and concentrate on writing. Maybe. Or maybe she'd never want to miss out on the exhilaration a live performance generated.

'I don't see any harm in an option. Though I warn you, I have no plans to sell. I think I've found a home and I plan to keep it.'

'But just in case.'

'Just in case.' She offered her hand, shook on the deal. 'So it's a truce, then?'

'Looks like it,' he replied.

'I'll pour the wine and we can drink to it. John-Michael, hand me three glasses, will you. The small ones. Sorry I don't have wine goblets.'

John-Michael got the designated glasses from the cupboard, darting a quick look at his father. Amanda intercepted it.

'It is all right with you if he has a wee bit?' she asked. She was not going to be put in the middle of something else.

'*One* will be all right, seeing as we are celebrating,' Mac replied.

'To our new truce.'

Dinner was quickly ready and on the small table in the dining area. The spaghetti sauce was thick and rich, drawing approval and praise from both males; the garlic bread crispy on the outside, soft and moist and garlicky on the inside; the fresh vegetable salad a sampler of vegetables in season.

Once the first hunger pangs had been satisfied, conversation again resumed. Topics discussed were general and non-controversial. Except when John-Michael again asked Amanda what she did for a living. She answered vaguely, and changed the subject. Mac watched her thoughtfully, but did not follow up on it. Amanda noticed his forbearance and was wont to clear up any misunderstandings, but not so in front of John-Michael. Mac still thought she was a hippie, putting her vague answers down to lack of a job. She wished now she had not let him have that opinion, had not been so childish as to try to score a point by not correcting him when he jumped to his erroneous conclusion. Would he understand her desire for privacy, understand why she went to such lengths to maintain it, why she was taking a long break from her work in the first place?

She was conscious throughout the meal of Mac's brooding gaze on her. Not only when she changed the topic of conversation from her career, from any job, but constantly. His eyes followed her throughout the evening. She licked her lips, tension rising as the night progressed; as she tried to ignore his constant surveillance, tried to concentrate on what John-Michael was discussing. To no avail. Amanda wanted to scream with self-consciousness. Did she have sauce smeared on her chin? Why was he so intense?

Dinner finally over, she quickly suggested they adjourned to the veranda for dessert. Twilight would soon fall, its faint light a shelter from Mac's constant watching. Amanda darted a quick glance at him again, her stomach flipping over as she clashed head on with his eyes. Mesmerised by the brilliant regard, she was entrapped, unable to tear her gaze away until Mac's eyes dropped to her mouth, as if reminding her of their exchange by the creek, the kisses . . .

'After dessert, we can play for Dad. I'll show what I've learned,' John-Michael said innocently.

Amanda looked at him questioningly, then smiled. Oh to be younger and unaware of the atmosphere, the tension in the air. She was the only one affected. No, a quick glance proved that, by the tight clenching of his jaw, Mac wasn't as unconcerned as he would like to appear. Amanda suddenly felt better.

When the evening was finally over and the MacKensies on their way home, Amanda couldn't determine if she was glad they had come, or happy the ordeal was over. She would have to take herself in hand when around Mac MacKensie. He still didn't approve wholeheartedly of her and she wasn't sure their new truce would prove to be the turning point in their relationship. Especially if he still considered her a hippie.

If the opportunity arose, she'd confide in Mac. The reason she wanted him to know the truth, of all the people in Timber, she refused to dwell on. She knew she could depend upon him not to tell anyone. But, if she could, she wanted to make sure the misunderstandings and falseness of her position were clarified.

Tuesday morning Amanda was up early. She whisked through the cabin in a quick clean and tidy campaign. She would be gone for almost two weeks and did not want to leave her place out of order. She glowed with pride as she worked. Her place. What a nice sound to it. As she polished the chrome on the sink, she reflected on the circumstances leading to her acquisition of her new home. That had been a most fortuitous day for her. To find a place right away and be able to buy it and move in within such a short time. What a stroke of luck. She had found the peace and relaxation she was looking for, and a new hobby. Panning for gold. She was again amused, remembering her cousin's reaction when he found out about it. Well, it would be something she could regale the band members with. Maybe they'd be amused too.

Shortly before John-Michael was due, she went to her bedroom window for the last look at her hill. The flowers would be past their prime soon, fading by the time she returned. Drinking in her fill, she gazed at the stately trees, the drying grass and undergrowth, just beginning to turn golden in the summer sun. She sighed and moved away. How silly, she was only going to be away for a week or so.

When the truck turned into the drive, she was ready. Casting a fond glance in farewell, she closed and locked the door.

'Hi, Mandy. This all?' John-Michael joined her on the veranda, motioning to her lone suitcase.

'Good morning, John-Michael. Yes, that's it. I'm only going for a few days.'

'I'll miss you.'

'Thank you, but you will have your guitar to practise, and work on the ranch. I'll be back soon and we can keep on with lessons, if you like.'

'Yes, I'd like. I'm glad you bought Cora's place.' He jerked the truck into gear and backed out.

They pulled out on to the highway just a short distance ahead of the bus travelling from Reno with the San Francisco destination emblazoned above the windscreen. John-Michael drew up before the depot just ahead of it.

'Do you have your ticket?' he asked, getting out to get the suitcase.

'No. I'll zip in and get it. Can you ask the bus to wait for me?'

'Sure, better hurry.'

Amanda dashed to the window, greeted the old man still working at the bus depot, and purchased her ticket. Her goodbye to John-Michael was, by necessity, hurried, as the bus had only a short stop in Timber.

'I'll meet you,' John-Michael said.

'Wonderful. Thanks. I'll be back Thursday week.'

'On the bus from San Francisco?'

'Yes, gets in just before noon, I think. Goodbye, John-Michael, thanks for bringing me in.' Amanda climbed aboard and waved.

In less than four hours the big bus was turning into its large, bustling, downtown San Francisco depot. Amanda waited for her luggage, then pushed through the crowd to the taxi stand on the street.

Phew, city life had certainly become more hectic since she was last here. She stood on the pavement, waiting for a cab to pull into the designated spot, watching the busy city moving around her. She shivered a little; San Francisco's famous fog was already coming in and the temperature was dropping quickly. In only a short time it would be cold, and she was not dressed for it.

'St Francis, please,' she said to the cab driver as she climbed into one that pulled into the taxi lane. She sank back against the seat, suitcase beside her, and watched out of the window at the crowded streets alive with cars, motorcycles, electric buses and bicycles. The pavements were full of people: wide-eyed tourists; stoic elderly Chinese women, weighed down by their packages; preoccupied businessmen in three-piece suits.

Grateful for the short distance between the depot and the Landmark Hotel on Union Square, Amanda soon reached her destination. Paying the driver, she glanced across Powell Street to Union Square, a small patch of green in a grey and cream forest of high-rises and tall towers. The few, neatly spaced trees were small and scrawny in the polluted city air. The rest of the view from the old hotel was of concrete and glass. Amanda sighed, homesick already for raw open land, few people and endless blue sky.

Stopping at the desk, she was informed she had already been registered and was sharing suite 1123. Amanda smiled her thanks, declined a porter for her lone bag, and, familiar with the hotel, went to the lifts. In only moments she stood knocking at the door of 1123.

Evie opened the door.

'Hi, Evie.'

'Mandy, hello, glad to see you!' Evie gave her a warm hug, calling over her shoulder, 'Here she is now, Davie, you can stop worrying.'

'Was Dave worried? How are you? And the baby?

You look enormous! Are you sure it is not coming tomorrow?'

Evie giggled delightedly. 'No, it's not coming for another month. I'm feeling fine now, though I get tired easily. I'm not going to Nashville with you this time because of it.'

Amanda widened her eyes at that. Since their marriage eighteen months earlier, Dave and Evie had rarely been separated. Even his recent visit to Timber had been extraordinary, and that only one night. Now they would be parted a week or more.

'Hi, coz.' Dave swept her up in a big hug, joining them in the small entry hallway. 'I wasn't worried,' he spoke to his wife as he released Amanda. 'Just wondering when she'd be here.'

'Sure you weren't honey.' Evie smiled and slipped her arm through his. 'Your room's through there, Mandy,' she said, pointing to the door on their right. The opposite wall held a duplicate door, to Evie and Dave's room.

Amanda and her cousin often shared a suite of rooms when travelling. It offered a central meeting area for the whole group, away from the public, where they could relax, plan or practise.

'Do you want to rest, or something?' Evie asked.

'No, I'm not tired. Let's go over the schedule so I know where we are.' Amanda dropped her bag near the door to her room and crossed into the living room, going to the sofa. 'We leave tomorrow, right? Arriving in Nashville late?'

'Right.' Dave joined her on the sofa as Evie sat on the arm. 'We'll get in late in the afternoon, so I didn't make any plans for tomorrow. Thursday morning we'll meet with Steve Potlack, discuss the new album. I've booked a few hours at the studio on Friday to cut one song if we want another demo. Which I doubt. Joe and Marc are already there. They'll be ready if we need anything.' Dave referred to two other members of the back-up band, the bass guitarist and the drummer. Joe's brother, Samuel, played electric piano and would fly east with Dave and Amanda.

'If the deal is signed with Steve, when will we record? I don't want to keep flying back and forth across the country all summer,' Amanda said.

'Me neither,' Dave gave Evie a fond look, 'especially when I become a father. We'll see how it goes. If Steve closes the deal on the terms we want, we will be using the studio in L.A. as you asked. It's only if he balks on that term that we have to try to negotiate something else. It's easier for him to come west once in a while than for all of us and all our gear to go east.'

'Sure,' Amanda laughed, 'he'll really buy that one. How often did we drive back and forth across the States doing concerts? It's a way of life for us. Try it anyway. I like the plan. L.A. I could take and not be away from my new home too much during my getaway summer.'

'We'll know for sure later this week. If he doesn't buy L.A., well, Nashville is only a few hours by plane.'

'I know. OK.'

Evie waited a moment, to see if either Amanda or Dave would continue the conversation. When they remained silent, she spoke.

'What have you done to your hair, Mandy?'

'What? Oh, I was trying to be less conspicuous, so I pulled it back. It's cooler in the hot weather, too.'

'Incognito's the word, toots,' Dave drawled, stretching his feet out and reaching for his wife's hand, threading his fingers through hers.

'But why?' Evie looked puzzled.

'So cousin Mandy could be loved for herself alone and not her money.' Dave's astute answer reminded Amanda of how close she and her cousin were, and always had been. She had not mentioned to him her desire to be liked for herself. He just knew her well.

'For true?' Evie asked Amanda.

'For true,' Amanda said solemnly. 'I'll fix it like I usually wear it tomorrow. I'm going to take a shower now. Can we eat Chinese food? I love it.'

'Sure.'

'Fine,' they said together, looked at each other and smiled.

Amanda swallowed a lump in her throat. It was so reassuring to find a couple still so much in love, still delighting in each other's company so much. One day, she thought, one day I'll have that, too. I hope. I'll have someone who will find delight in my presence, whom I will want to spend my time with. The words to her song flashed into her head. Slowly she got up.

'Won't be long, then let's go eat.'

Heads turned the next day when Amanda walked briskly through the new north terminal at the San Francisco International Airport. She was dressed in a fashionable denim trouser suit and leather boots. Her hair was gleaming, clean and shiny, cascading around her face, on her shoulders, part way down her back. Skilfully applied make-up highlighted and enhanced the natural beauty of her bright blue eyes. She carried a leather shoulder bag, and walked through the terminal with the confident air of someone who knows where they are going, oblivious to the stares, nudges and whispers going on around her. In truth, preoccupied with the forthcoming journey.

She checked in at the designated gate just after the boarding had commenced. Dave would join her in a few moments. He was seeing Evie off on her plane to Los Angeles. Scanning the crowd as she moved towards the jetway, Amanda wondered where Sam was. Perhaps on board already.

'Seen Sam?' Dave joined her.

'Hi. No, maybe he's on board. Evie off OK?'

'Yeah. Wish she were coming with us this trip,' he said, looking a little lost.

Amanda patted his arm. 'It won't be so long.'

Sam was already in his seat, across the aisle from the two booked for Amanda and Dave. He greeted the others, indicating he would trade places with Dave later in the flight to spend some of the travel time with Amanda.

It was a long, boring flight. Amanda had made it several times in the last few years, always on business. She would talk part of the time with her cousin, part of the time with Sam, to catch up on family news, go over some of the business that had cropped up in her absence.

Dave brought up business first. They discussed the forthcoming visit in further detail and the possibilities it opened, the terms they wanted and some of the possible songs for the new album. Dave complimented Amanda on the ones she had most recently written, at Timber. They had tried them with the band and both had sounded good.

'What about your rancher?' he asked next.

'What about him?' she asked, growing still.

'I'm not asking you that. You tell me.'

'He's not "my rancher", as you put it.'

'Do you want him to be?'

Amanda was silent a long time, staring out the window at the empty sky. 'I'm not sure,' she answered slowly. 'I do want to get married, to find someone to have a very special relationship with. To love, to have love me.' She smiled at Dave. 'Like you and Evie have.'

'And give up all this?' He waved his hand.

'No, not all. I don't think I will want to travel as much in the future. It gets tiring. But I don't want to give it up totally. Still sing and travel some. Just not so much. That's not so outrageous, is it?'

'I could handle that, especially with a baby soon. Evie won't be able to travel with me as much.'

'I could take more time to write songs. I really like that part, Davie.'

'It's where you started, what you're good at. In addition to the singing. of course. But the rancher?'

'I don't know. I find him very attractive, very sexy. I like being around him, but he is so hard to get anywhere with.' Suddenly the kiss by the stream flashed into her mind. She would like to know Mac more, maybe. But you didn't pin hopes for a long-lasting love on someone who treats you distastefully, no matter how attracted you were physically ... did you?

She shrugged. 'Time enough, I guess. What are we doing for the album?'

'We like the ones you just wrote. They should both go. *Bluebells on the Hills* is the one that needs just a little more work.'

'Yes, I know. I thought it would help to hear it with the band, see better just where it was weak.'

'Lyrics are nice.'

She bowed her head. 'Thanks, coz. I think I'm ready to settle down.'

'So your song says. Me, too.' Dave was silent for a moment. 'It's been grand fun, though.'

'Sure, and will still be, only not so much travel.'

The big plane droned on, flying eastward towards the Great Smokey mountains of Tennessee, towards the fertile green basin of Nashville. Dave swapped seats with Sam. He and Amanda flew the last hour together, talking of family. Sam had taken a few weeks to visit in Colorado and was bringing Amanda up to date on everything from their home town.

Joe and Marc met the plane, greeting the travellers,

taking them to the hotel where they had already reserved rooms. It was located near the famous Renshaw Theatre, first home of the Grand Ole Opry.

Amanda didn't even see the city as they drove through it. She had been here many times now and no longer stood in awe. She was here to do a job. Work and then go home. She had neither the time nor inclination for tourism.

CHAPTER EIGHT

AMANDA was tired, but feeling the stirrings of excitement as the bus drew near Timber. Her trip had been short and hectic, not the least of which had been this final leg. Up early yesterday, to fly from Nashville to Los Angeles. Making arrangements to have some furniture shipped from L.A. to her cabin had kept her busy in the afternoon. Then, up early again this morning to catch the flight to San Francisco in time to connect with the bus. What with the time zone differences, irregular meals and heavy schedule in Nashville, she was worn out. She hoped John-Michael would remember to pick her up.

She was still attired as she had been for the last week; hair freshly washed, wavy and soft in the bright sun, make-up tastefully applied, highlighting her natural beauty. Her dark blue brushed denim trouser suit was not suitable for summer travelling in California's hot central valley, but had been welcome for San Francisco's cool, foggy climate, and would not be too heavy for the cooler mountain air. Fortunately, the bus was air-conditioned.

Familiar landmarks sparked recognition. She recalled this stretch of highway. Soon they'd round a bend, see the river and traverse the bridge. Next stop, Timber!

As they pulled into the petrol station depot, Amanda saw the grey truck parked near the building. Gathering her few things from her seat, she glimpsed John-Michael standing against the truck, waiting. He had remembered! Thank goodness. Almost home how.

When she stepped from the vehicle, her heart

caught in her throat. Mac MacKensie was the person leaning back against the bonnet of the battered old truck, hat low on his face, arms crossed. Waiting.

She swallowed hard, her heart tripping at the sight of him. Summoning up a smile, she walked over.

'Hi.'

'Have a good trip?' He took in her appearance, his eyes wandering slowly from her hair to her fancy boots.

'Yes, thanks.'

He glanced at her face. 'Come into an inheritance?'

'No. Is, uh, did John-Michael come?'

'Nope. I will give you a lift home.'

'Thank you. I have a few more cases this time.'

He shrugged and moved to open the door. 'Climb in and I'll get them. You're the only one off the bus, I take it all the baggage will be yours.'

Glancing back, Amanda realised the driver was already unloading her things from the luggage area. Everything looked familiar.

'It looks like it. I'll help.'

'I can manage. Just get in.'

'Yes, sir!' She gave a mock salute, stopping Mac in his tracks as he turned towards the bus. When he glared at her, Amanda giggled, gave a saucy wink and promptly climbed into the cab.

She watched as Mac gathered her things and loaded them in the truck. Her eyes feasted on him. She had almost forgotten how tall he was, how broad his shoulders were. His hat, pulled low on his forehead, hid most of the bronzed hair, though she could see it gleaming in the sun when his back was to her.

He was certainly an attractive man, in spite of the stern look perpetually on his face. No, she remembered how he looked when he smiled. He should do it more often. Could she make him?

The last box in the truck, he joined her in the cab,

the look from his green eyes almost like an electric shock. He stared her for a long, charged moment, at last moving to start the engine.

'You look nice,' he said, turning the wheel to take the pick-up from the parking lot. 'A little tired, though.'

'I am tired,' she replied. 'Thank you for picking me up. Where's John-Michael?'

'Home.'

'Was it inconvenient for him to come for me?'

Mac threw her a look. 'Object to me?'

'No, of course not. I just . . . I mean I was expecting John-Michael.' What was the matter with her? She had just negotiated and signed a large recording contract; started preliminaries for a concert tour in the autumn; travelled across the country and back; made arrangements to have furniture delivered and was now stammering like a teenager. Taking a deep breath, she slowly released it.

'I had to come to town, so I picked you up. I wanted to see you.'

Amanda's heart gave a small skip. Mac had wanted to see her! Her face broke into a lovely smile as she shifted a little in the seat, relaxing a little.

He spoke again. 'Why so much stuff this time? You hit a jackpot or something?'

'No. I have an apartment in L.A. and I'm bringing things back here to really make my cabin a home. I was only planning to check out the area when I came before. Then I saw Cora's place and stayed.'

'Without further investigation?' He looked disapproving.

She shrugged. 'It was a wild splurge. I saw something I liked and took it. Haven't you ever done anything like that?'

'What if you didn't like it here? What if you found it was a mistake to move to Timber? Did you consider that?'

'No, not at all. If I don't like it, I'll leave. I can always change my mind. I'm not hurting anyone. Not responsible to anyone for how I live my life. I certainly won't do or not do something just because of other people's views.'

'Hippies always see themselves as free souls, beholden to no one. Live their lives however they choose. Irresponsible, that's all,' Mac said.

'Not only hippies,' she retorted quickly. 'Others choose to live their lives as they want. All people who are working at something they like, who live where they want, are doing the same thing. That doesn't make them irresponsible. Aren't you glad you are a rancher?'

'Of course I am. But I didn't buy a place on impulse, without checking into it.'

'But I did,' she replied sweetly, 'and I'll do it again if I choose.'

'Oh, so we're rich now, are we? Where are you buying your next place?'

'I'd do it again,' she rephrased. 'Why did you want to see me?'

'I came to see you last Thursday. I didn't realise you had gone anywhere. John-Michael didn't mention it until I asked him. I have that option agreement we discussed.'

Amanda's face fell. She felt like a pricked balloon. He only wanted to see her so they could lock up the option agreement. He hadn't really wanted to see her, except to ensure his hold on her property. She was so disappointed she wanted to cry, to renege on the option and let him worry if she'd ever sell to him or not. More fool her for thinking he wanted to see her for any reason other than business. Well, so be it.

'OK. I'll look at it,' she said, suddenly tired again. She fell silent for the remainder of the ride.

In spite of her disappointment, when they rounded

the bend to her track, she felt a lifting of spirits. Her
cabin looked so small and isolated after the massive,
crowded high-rises and glass edifices of the cities. The
soaring pines, the faded green grassy meadows, the
quiet breeze were soothing to jangled nerves, giving a
pervading sense of tranquillity to a weary traveller.

Amanda was glad to be home. To be home with no
necessity to go away again until the summer was over.
She would relax, spend time decorating her home, and
writing songs. It would be a wonderful summer and
she was determined to enjoy every minute of it. In
spite of her disapproving neighbour.

As soon as Mac stopped, Amanda climbed out,
going to the back of the truck and pulling one of her
cases from it.

'I will get those,' Mac said, lifting two other cases.

'I can help,' she said, heading for the door. Amanda
carried her case directly through to her bedroom. She
flung open the window, silently greeting the hills, the
trees, and her bluebells on the hill, now waning. When
she re-entered the living room a few moments later,
Mac was setting down a box she had brought, the last
of her baggage.

Crossing to the front window, she opened it for
cross-ventilation. Taking off her jacket, she laid it and
her sun-glasses on the table.

'Did you get a job?' Mac asked, watching her.

'I may have something lined up. For the fall,' she
replied, shrugging.

'I wondered, you look all fixed up. For an
interview?'

Amanda's hackles rose again. She had forgotten for
a moment he thought her a hippie. It was such a
different impression than most people had about her.
An imp of mischief took over. Giving him a big grin,
she turned around.

'Do you like it? I bought some other things, too,

now that I'm moving in for good.' She opened her eyes wide and stared limpidly up at him.

'Where did you get the money for all this finery?'

'Here and there.' She waved her hand vaguely.

'Doing something you shouldn't, I warrant. Did it involve that nefarious man you had spend the night a while back?'

'Nefarious man? You mean Dave?' Amanda gave a small giggle. 'Dave is not nefarious. He's my cousin.'

'I bet!'

'Where's the option agreement?' She would change the subject before it got any worse.

'Here.' Mac drew an envelope from his pocket and handed it to her.

Amanda opened it and scanned the page. It looked pretty standard to her, but she'd read it carefully before signing. The amount for purchase of the option was blank. She looked up questioningly.

'We never discussed the money. My attorney drew up the agreement and left that blank. There should be some remittance for the option. How much?' Mac asked.

Still piqued that he had only come for her to clear up the option, she replied carelessly, 'Five thousand.'

'You're nuts!' he thundered. 'I'm not paying for your life here in Timber! You find your income somewhere else. You want a job, I'll help you get one, but you're not riding free on my money.'

Amanda smiled. My, he was quick-tempered. Could she always make him mad so easily she wondered, tilting her head consideringly.

'Too high, eh?'

'A damn sight too high. I say one hundred dollars.'

'OK,' she replied instantly, amiably.

Mac stared at her a long moment, reading the laughter in her eyes. Slowly relaxing until the glimmer of a smile touched his lips.

'I ought to spank you.'

'Doesn't sound like fun. I'll read the agreement tonight and bring it up tomorrow. I'm tired and want to eat and go to bed.'

'All right. Fair enough. I'll be home in the morning.'

'OK. Thanks again for bringing me home. I guess I'm going to have to get a car or something. This place is just too far to walk to town for everything.'

'Yes. Before I forget, Elizabeth instructed me to invite you for dinner next Wednesday. She's having a few people in and wanted you to join them.'

'Where does she live?'

'Not too far from here. Oh, no car. I can give you a lift. John-Michael and I are going, too. No trouble.'

Amanda nodded, certain Mac would not have offered if it were any trouble.

'Do you have a, uh . . . dress?'

'Yes, of course.' She gave him an exasperated look. 'Don't you worry, I won't let your aunt down. What time?'

'About seven. We'll be by a little before.'

'OK. Tell John-Michael hi for me, will you?'

'Yes.' Mac turned, pulled his hat down firmly and opened the door, pausing to throw a glance back at Amanda. 'Glad you're back, spitfire.'

'I'll bet,' she mimicked.

Up early the next morning, Amanda waited until after ten before walking up to Mac's home to give him the signed option agreement. She had read it carefully the night before. It was clear-cut and straightforward: if and when she ever sold the property, in exchange for the $100 Mac would give her, she would give him first refusal to buy the property at fair market value.

Amanda saw nothing wrong with it, signed it and was now carrying it up to return to Mac. The gravel roadway wound upward through the tall trees.

Rustlings in the undergrowth and the birds chirping their own melodies reminded Amanda she was not alone on her walk, even though she didn't see another creature. What a pleasant way of life. She did like cities for the cultural advantages they offered, but she loved the country.

The wooden bridge traversing the creek did not seem any more substantial to Amanda than it had before. She walked quickly across it, watching her step. Shaky though it appeared, it was solid and did not move at all under her slight weight. That obstacle behind her, she continued briskly up the drive.

She was dressed in her inevitable jeans and T-shirt, hair drawn back in a ribbon and glasses firmly in position. Since she had received a reprieve yesterday with Mac picking her up instead of John-Michael, she had decided not to tempt fate. Her 'disguise' was back in place.

Cresting the last hill, Amanda paused as she again took in the view from the homesite. The endless mountains, rising in the distance, a little blurry today. To the left, in the far distance, a stately snow-capped peak rose loftily above the tree line. Amanda gazed out for endless moments, spellbound by the sheer beauty of the vista.

Slowly, reluctantly, she turned towards the house. It was in a wonderful location. If it were hers, she'd spend hours on the veranda, just staring out over the land. Did Mac ever do that? Did he share any of her feelings about the mountains? Or just take it all for granted, never aware of the sheer beauty, the mighty majesty of the Sierra Nevada range?

Mac answered the door to her knock. There was no loud music blaring this time, only the soft swish of the breeze through the grass and trees.

'Hallo.' His look quickly took in her attire.

'Hi. I brought the option letter.'

'Back to mountain dress, I see,' he commented.

She shrugged. 'It's comfy. Do I come in, or just hand it over to you and leave?' She offered the paper.

Stepping aside, he opened the door wider. As she passed by, he took the proferred paper, opening it and verifying she had signed. He closed the door, resting back against it, watching Amanda closely.

She felt her pulse quicken with the sound of the latch. She was in Mac's house on the hill. Alone?

'Where's John-Michael?' she asked, in what she hoped was a casual tone.

'Down at the barn. You walked up?'

'Of course.' She would not be intimidated by his eyes. She took off her glasses and moved to the large window. The view was even better from this position.

'Thought maybe your friend from the other night might have given you a lift.'

'Dave? He doesn't live around here.'

'Did you see him on your trip?' Mac left the door to join her near the window.

'We travelled together.'

'I bet you did.'

Amanda felt the tug at the back of her head, then her hair fell free on her shoulders. She spun round to find herself very close to Mac. He was dangling the ribbon.

'Give it back.'

'Why not leave it down? It looks nice that way.'

'It's too hot.' She reached for the ribbon, but he held it away from her.

'It's not hot in here. Pleasant, I thought.'

'Come on, Mac.'

'Come and get it,' he invited softly.

Amanda glared at him a moment, then put on a deliberately sweet expression, moving close to him, looking up nicely into his face, eyes blazing. 'Please Mac, give my ribbon to me,' she said.

He smiled sardonically. 'How artificial.'

Moving quickly, he pulled her into his arms, his face blotting out all else as his mouth claimed hers. Amanda was startled, not expecting his embrace. Before she could protest, however, his arms pulled her tight against him, moulding her body to his, his lips warm and persuasive against hers, the contact with his body sending waves of desire and longing through her. One touch of his mouth and she was lost.

As the kiss deepened, Amanda was vaguely aware of Mac's hand in her hair, running his fingers through the long tresses, gently rubbing the nape of her neck. She shivered with delight, a lassitude taking hold, her body growing weak. Gratefully she clung to Mac for support. His hands pulled up her T-shirt, caressing the bare skin beneath it. Slowly his lips moved against hers, his tongue penetrating the moist softness of her mouth, his hands warm and exciting against her bare skin.

Amanda was floating on waves of sweet pleasure. Her heart began beating heavily in her breast as she grew breathless with the feelings Mac could evoke. She moved closer still, pressing against him, moving easily in his arms as he tilted her head back and trailed kisses down her throat, back to her mouth. His hands warm and gentle on her skin, in her hair, rubbing her back, tracing her spine, up and down. Now moving along her ribs, his thumb beneath the elastic of her bra, caressing the swell of her breast. Amanda's arms locked together around his neck as she tried to move closer, to stop the tantalising touch of his hand, to slow the fire building within her. He held her away, his hands continuing their wanderings, his mouth hot and firm and sweet against hers. The moments floated by.

Suddenly Mac broke away, pulling his hands

abruptly from her. At the same second, Amanda heard a familiar voice.

'Dad . . .' John-Michael entered the room from the front door, surprise held him silent only a moment, then a big grin lit his face.

'Hi, Mandy. I see you are back.'

Blushing like a schoolgirl, she tried a weak smile. 'Hi, John-Michael. Yes, I'm back.'

She did not look at Mac. In fact, Amanda didn't know where to look. Maybe she could just jump out of the window and end it all.

Mac moved to his desk and rummaged through some papers. 'I believe I owe you a cheque.'

'Wow, Mandy, you must be good!' John-Michael teased, laughing as she blushed again.

'John-Michael!' Mac's voice was thunderous.

'Yeah?' He was still smiling.

'What are you doing here?'

'Dad, I live here.'

'Don't get smart. I mean now. I thought you were going to exercise the two horses.'

'That's why I'm here. Jookie's thrown a shoe. I did exercise the bay.'

'Leave Jookie for the day, then.'

'I planned to, until he got another shoe. I came up for lunch.'

Amanda put her glasses back in place and retrieved the ribbon, tying back her hair as she turned her back on the two males and looked out of the window. Her eyes were blind to the view, however. She was embarrassed to be caught in such circumstances. She should not have been such a willing participant, though she could still feel Mac's hands on her, her breath coming more quickly at the remembrances. She hadn't felt like this before.

How funny John-Michael must view them. His Dad and the new neighbour. She smiled a little. High drama it was not. Living on a ranch, he would not be unaware of the physical aspects. For a moment, Amanda wished she was unaware of them. Mac was damnably attractive. She took a deep breath.

'Here you go.'

Turning, she saw Mac standing several safe feet away, cheque extended.

Suppressing a smile, she reached for it, scanned it. One hundred dollars.

'Thank you.' She risked a quick look to his face; it was closed. 'I will remind you, I don't plan to sell any time soon.'

'I know. Maybe you'll change your mind.'

'I'll come for a lesson today or tomorrow, if it's all right,' John-Michael said.

'Fine. Whenever. I'll be home, or at the creek.'

She folded the cheque and stuffed it into her jeans' pocket.

'Do you want a ride home?' Mac asked, still standing several feet away.

It was tempting. Maybe he would drive her and ... 'No, it's a nice walk. Downhill, too, this time.'

'See you later, Mandy.'

'Bye, John-Michael, Mac.' She left, head held high.

It was Sunday afternoon before John-Michael appeared. Amanda heard the horse and went to greet him when he did arrive.

'Hi.'

'Hi. I hope it is convenient for a lesson,' he asked diffidently.

'Sure.'

Joining her on the veranda, he seemed more unsure of himself than before.

'Before we start, I'm sorry if I was out of line teasing the other day. Dad gave me hell for it,' John-Michael said, fingering his guitar awkwardly.

'No problem. Your dad over-reacted. He shouldn't have said anything. I knew you were teasing.'

'He's been like a bear with a sore head these last few days. Worse than before.' He gave her a sly look. 'Wouldn't like to come up and charm him out of it, would you?'

'Watch it, John-Michael, or no more lessons. I irritate your father as much as you say you do, if not lots more.'

'Didn't seem like it the other day.'

'John-Michael!'

'OK, OK. I've practised while you were gone. See if I've improved.' He sat down on one of the frayed porch chairs, put his guitar in place, and began playing. Amanda could see a definite improvement. It was heartening for a teacher to have such an apt pupil.

'You are doing very well.' She spoke warmly when he had finished. 'Let's go on.'

She taught him more chords, new timing and listed out several new songs to practise.

When he was leaving, John-Michael paused. 'You ride, don't you?'

'Sure do.'

'Want to go on a picnic tomorrow? Just with me? I know a nice field where we can eat. It has a nice view.'

'I'm a sucker for nice views, and good companionship. I'd like to go. Shall I come late morning?'

'Yes, or I can bring a horse here.'

'No, I'll walk up, meet you there. What shall I bring?'

'Nothing. I'll fix the lunch. Thank you for the lesson. Thanks for all the lessons.'

'You're welcome, John-Michael. I'll see you tomorrow.'

She waved to John-Michael as he rode away, his words from earlier echoing in her head. So Mac was in a bad temper, was he? Disappointed at the interrup-

tion? Amanda frowned. If he were, why not come and
see her? He certainly knew where she lived. Maybe
John-Michael was exaggerating, or maybe Mac was
only upset at being caught dallying with Timber's
'resident hippie'. She had better get that cleared up.
But how? Just come out and say, I'm not a hippie. I'm
a country singer and make tons of money and am
known all over the country? No. She'd wait until it
came up casually, naturally, in conversation.

CHAPTER NINE

JOHN-MICHAEL, bulging saddle-bags slung over one shoulder, led the way from the big house to the barn the next morning when Amanda arrived. The barn was large, with lofts towering above the stalls, hay from last winter still remaining. When the summer's harvest was in, it would again be filled to its rafters, enough hay for feed all winter.

'Jessie's a good one.' John-Michael stopped beside a stall, looking over the rail at the brown mare gravely staring back. One white streak blazed down her face. 'I'll saddle her for you.'

Amanda took a deep breath, savouring the mingled scents of hay, horse and manure. It brought back a hundred-and-one memories.

'I can manage, if you show me the tack.' She had ridden since she was five.

'Sure. Here's a halter. We can take them to the rail near the tack room, less distance to carry all the gear.'

'A man after my own heart,' Amanda said easily. 'Lead on.' She competently put the halter on the docile mare, snapped on a lead line and opened the stall.

John-Michael had brought out his chestnut and was leading him to the opposite end of the barn from where they had entered. Amanda followed, through the large opening, then to the left. Immediately adjacent to the barn was the tack room, a hitching rail before it. Tethering the horses, John-Michael showed Amanda where the tack was. In only minutes, both were busy saddling the horses.

'Oh, oh,' John-Michael said softly. 'Here comes trouble.'

'What?' Amanda looked up as Mac rode into the yard, stopping behind the chestnut gelding, dispassionately regarding them.

'Hi, Dad,' John-Michael said.

Mac nodded, his eyes on Amanda.

She licked her lips, conscious of his regard, and continued her activity, feeling suddenly awkward and clumsy.

'Going riding?' Mac asked.

'Yes. Thought I'd show Mandy around. Have a picnic up near the point.'

'I see.' Mac continued to watch them. The silence stretched out endlessly.

Amanda finished first, but was in no hurry to draw attention to the fact. Before John-Michael was ready, however, Mac spoke again.

'Mind if I join you?'

John-Michael looked up in surprise, then pleasure filled his face. 'Sure Dad, glad to have you.' He paused. 'I guess we will have enough food for three.'

'I won't eat much.'

'Oh, I'm sure there's plenty.' John-Michael was ready. He led his horse away from the rail and mounted. Mac remained where he was, watching Amanda.

'Need any help?' he asked. 'You mount from the left.'

She threw him a scathing look. 'I know.'

Leading her horse a few steps from the rail, she double checked the cinch, and mounted. It had been a year or more since she had last ridden, her last visit home to Colorado. But one never forgot. She loved riding, and wondered suddenly why she had not done much of it in the last few years. The pressures of work were not so demanding she could not have spared some time for riding.

'Oh, yes. You're a ranch gal, I forgot,' Mac murmured, drawing up beside her as they left the barn yard and began descending along a trail that skirted one of the pastures. John-Michael was in the lead.

'I was raised on one in Colorado.'

'Gave it up for the carefree hippie life in San Francisco, eh? Ranching is hard work.'

'I'm not against hard work . . .' she began. Was now the time to tell him what she did, why she had taken her trip? He interrupted and the moment was gone.

'As long as it's someone else's and you can just sit around and make beautiful music.'

'Some people like music,' she snapped.

'Sure, but for entertainment and relaxation once their work is finished for the day.'

'Someone has to make it for other people to enjoy.'

'Hey, you two, come on.' John-Michael was a dozen yards or more ahead, turned in his saddle. 'Thought you wanted to see the place, Mandy, not fight with Dad.'

Amanda urged her horse forward, catching up.

'Yes, I do. Sorry, but your father . . .' She shook her head.

'We mustn't offend our guest's gentle sensibilities,' Mac said joining them. 'From now on, I'll be the model host and guide. Please note on your left is a five acre pasture. It will support over ten head of horses during our growing season, with supplements. We have irrigation for continuous growth of grass during the summer months. Ahead is another pasture.'

The tour of the ranch was thorough and informative, though once or twice Amanda suspected Mac was deliberately throwing facts and figures so furiously at her to try to overwhelm her. She listened intently, concentrating on keeping it all straight, in spite of him. All the numbers she could not be expected to remember; the basics of ranching she was already familiar with. It wasn't all that difficult.

John-Michael led the way when the trail began to narrow. Amanda followed with Mac bringing up the rear. Curving through the trees, switching back as the terrain grew steeper, the trail cut through the undergrowth. In some places, the branches and leaves met across their path, the horses forcing them apart as they continued their plodding climb.

The air was cool in the dappled shade, a small breeze ruffling the uppermost limbs of the Ponderosas. Birds fluttered, chattered; squirrels and mysterious rustling in the undergrowth could be heard now that conversation was impossible. Amanda's heart swelled with happiness. She loved this land, she loved riding. Maybe she could get a horse, if she could arrange her travel schedule to warrant enough usage to justify the expense. Maybe she could even work out some arrangement with Mac for boarding the horse.

She stifled a laugh at that. She could imagine how co-operative he would be to make her life more appealing in Timber, when all he wanted was for her to leave so he could obtain her land. No, she'd have to find another solution.

'We're here,' John-Michael called.

The riders burst forth from the trees, into the bright, sunlit open field, surrounded on three sides by the thick Sierra forest. On the fourth side the meadow ended in a sheer drop; beyond, only sky and endless mountains and valleys to the south of the field.

'Oh!' Amanda's eyes lit up with the sight. It was magnificent. Involuntarily she stopped her horse, just gazing at the smoky mounds in the distance. In one valley a suspicious glint of light suggested a river or lake.

John-Michael dismounted, tethering his horse. Mac

followed suit, looking to Amanda, still enthralled with the view.

'Need help?' he asked, reaching up to grasp her by the waist.

'I can manage,' she protested, as the warmth of his fingers penetrated her shirt, his strength against her body. It seemed effortless, the ease with which he lifted her from the saddle and set her down on the grass. Amanda could feel her heart race with his nearness. She kept her eyes fixed on his throat, the brown column rising from his blue-checked shirt, the pulse at the base strong and steady.

'Thanks.' She didn't recognise the thready voice as her own. She took a deep breath to strengthen it. Stepping back, she was reluctant to break contact, still was realistic enough to realise safety lay in distance.

'You're welcome.' A trace of amusement in the timbre.

'Can I help unpack?' Amanda joined John-Michael. He had already pulled his saddle-bags from his mount and was moving towards a flat area nearby.

'We can just pull it all out and start eating.'

Amanda settled herself on the warm grass, the forest behind her, the view before her. Contentedly, she sat in the blazing sun, munching on a sandwich as she gazed off into the distance, not talking, only half listening as John-Michael and Mac exchanged remarks.

Replete from eating, Amanda's eyes began to grow heavier, the balmy air and hot sun joining to make her positively sleepy. Slowly she sank back upon the scented grass, her lids closing, the warmth of the sun a gentle blanket, the breeze moving softly against her skin, keeping the sun from being too hot. Amanda drifted off to sleep.

'But Dad, there's got to be some time when it is

OK. What about secret agents? You don't think they can function without deceit.'

Gradually Amanda was becoming aware of the man and boy talking. Bit by bit she became more awake. She remained lying down, idly listening, not at first understanding the trend of the conversation, still dozing.

Mac hadn't replied immediately to John-Michael's comment. When he did, Amanda had almost forgotten what John-Michael had said.

'Probably most of our problems in the world today are due to deceit of one form or another. But, I grant you, due to the way things are, it is necessary for a spy or whatever you want to call him to be deceitful. But that doesn't apply to day-to-day living, especially here in Timber. Deception is wrong, John-Michael, it is not a basis for any kind of interaction.'

'I still think it is OK in some circumstances,' he muttered.

Mac caught it. 'Like what?' he asked sharply.

'I don't know. Like if you really didn't like a lady's dress and she asks you, so you say it is pretty or something.'

'That's hardly the same thing, though a really clever person can come up with an honest reply which won't insult or hurt the lady. I suspect I'm rather rigid in my views on this, but there it is. A person is either straightforward or not. Ones that are not, aren't to be trusted. Better to stay away from them. I have very little tolerance for lies and deception.'

'Me, too, Dad. Only sometimes it might be justified. That's all I'm trying to say.'

'Umm.' Mac's reply was non-committal.

'I'm going to Billy Oldmyer's house next week. They are having a big barbecue. I think most of the guys from school are going. Good chance to see them all again. It seems like a long time since school got out.' John-Michael changed the subject.

Amanda lost track of the conversation, caught up in Mac's words on lies and deceit, wondering what had been the starting point of the conversation, why they were discussing deceit in the first place. What would he think when he knew her position here now was based on a lie by omission? She wanted to share with him her reasons for not letting neighbours know who she was, but now wondered if she could, and still maintain some sort of friendly relationship. He seemed so very adamant against deceit of any sort. On the other hand, she could not envisage herself adhering to this role for years just because of his views. Once she knew some people, and they accepted her for herself, she had no objection to the whole world knowing what she did for a living. She was proud of her work, of her accomplishments. It was just initially that she did not want those accomplishments to affect her acceptance in the community.

What a quandary. She wanted Mac to think well of her. Why, she refused to closely examine. If she wanted to clear it up, she had better do it soon. Before it got worse.

With the decision made, she stretched, coming fully awake, and slowly sat up.

'Gosh, Sleepyhead, we thought you'd sleep all afternoon?' John-Michael said.

'Your snoring scared all the animals off,' Mac said.

'I don't snore,' she replied disdainfully.

'How do you know?' John-Michael asked.

'Someone must have told her,' Mac replied, his eyes watching her.

She gave him a very speaking glance, unaware it had no effect because her sunglasses hid her face. 'Someone did, as a matter of fact,' she said sweetly, 'my sister.'

'I didn't know you had a sister,' John-Michael said with interest.

'Oh, yes. I'm one of five, two girls and three boys. Plus, my mother is from a large family, my dad's from a large family and their brothers and sisters also married people from big families. I had forty-three cousins within a ten mile radius of town.'

'Gosh, I'm an only child; Dad is too. I don't know about my mother.'

'She had a sister, but no kids there, last I heard,' Mac said, gathering up the remnants of lunch. 'I've work to do. Are you two heading back now?'

'Yes. I've some things to do, too. It's been lovely, though. Thanks for asking me, John-Michael. You have a beautiful place.

'Glad you like it, Mandy. Come and ride any time. That's OK with you, isn't it Dad?'

Mac was quiet for a moment and Amanda couldn't resist, 'Thinking up an honest answer that won't insult me, Mac?'

'Eavesdropping, were you?'

She grinned easily. 'Only the last few minutes, just as I was waking. Don't worry. I won't come riding if I'm not wanted,' she said with scarcely any pang.

'I'll go with you a few times, make sure you can find your way around; and don't neglect or abuse my horses.'

'Charming.' She stood, reconsidered. 'Thank you, I might like it after all.' The two of them, alone, riding; what better opportunity for sharing confidences?

Mac left them before they reached the barn, riding across the field, erect, yet at ease in the saddle, his hat low on his face to protect from the sun.

Amanda watched until he was lost from view. It had been a nice day, made even more so by Mac's unexpected arrival. John-Michael was waiting for her when she turned back.

'Tell me about growing up with forty-three cousins. It must have been fun.'

'Oh, it was. We are all close, some of each age, you know, so everyone has someone special. Holidays are the best. Aunt Meg has the biggest place, so we almost always go there for Christmas.' Amanda recounted holidays on the ride to the barn. John-Michael listened with great interest, asking questions, laughing, sharing her memories wistfully.

'How did you ever leave?' he asked as they unsaddled the horses.

'Well, a couple of us work together, try to get home a few times each year, though it's been a while since we've been back this last stretch. The others are all grown, too. Some married and moved away. We still see each other whenever we can. It was great fun and I loved it. But I like California, too. This is where I want my home, for my kids to have happy memories.'

'Yeah, I guess so.' John-Michael was quiet as he brushed down his mount, led him to the corral and turned him loose inside. Amanda was right behind him.

As they watched the horses amble away, he spoke again, pensively. 'I guess if Dad and Mom had stayed together, there would have been more kids. It's hard to imagine, though.'

'Your father is still fairly young. He could marry again, have more.'

'Wouldn't be the same. I'm almost grown now. Well, maybe I wouldn't have liked sharing anyway. Want to come to the house for a Coke?'

'No, thank you, some other time if I may. I've had a fun time today. Thank you for asking me. It's a great ranch, John-Michael. I would like to come again.'

'Sure, any time. I might come tomorrow for another lesson.'

'Good. See you then.' With a smile and wave, she was off.

CHAPTER TEN

AMANDA dressed with great care for Elizabeth Burke's dinner party. She had not seen Mac since the picnic. John-Michael had come for another lesson, not referring to the picnic, nor to the embrace he had interrupted, but smiling at Amanda more than before. She, of course, did not refer to either; what could she say? Besides, the interrupted embrace had only been a kiss. Only a kiss? She grew warm all over whenever she thought about it. Well, then, maybe a little more than just a kiss.

Amanda decided to throw caution to the wind and really dress for dinner. If someone recognised her, all right. If not, she would at least look her best. She washed and curled her hair, brushing it until it gleamed, soft and wavy around her face. Make-up was subtly donned, enhancing her blue eyes and high cheek bones, yet not overtly put on. She wanted to look especially nice. For the other guests, she told herself, thinking of a particular 'other guest'. To erase the hippie image, if she could.

Her dress was a soft, creamy jersey, with high ruffled collar, long sleeves with ruffles capturing her wrists. It clung to her figure, outlining her firm breasts, slender waist and rounded hips. Amanda was pleased to see she had put on a little weight since her summer began. She had been too thin at the end of her last tour.

One last glance in the mirror convinced her she was ready. The dress swayed gently as she walked, moulding her slight frame, displaying her figure to advantage as she moved. Mac would be here soon to pick her up. She would not need to keep him waiting. Nervously she fingered her skirt, then chided herself for her foolishness. She, who had performed many times before thousands of people, was nervous of a man coming to pick her up to drive her to a small dinner party. Honestly! One would think it mattered.

Gazing out the window with sightless eyes, Amanda paused. It did matter. She was anxious that he should like her. Maybe more than like her. She wanted it to be for herself, however. For Mac to value her for what she was, not for the fame she had achieved. In a moment's conversation she could clear up the hippie image, could clear up any misconceptions about her situation, chance his anger about deceit and let him know she was a hard-working, successful member of society.

But, still, stubbornly, Amanda clung to the notion of being wanted for herself, as she was, not for what she had accomplished. Wanted him to want her as he knew her. Let the explanations come later. Sighing softly, she wondered if it were a pipe-dream. Was it worth it?

She heard the truck before she saw it turn into the drive. Only it wasn't the old grey truck, but a gleaming maroon and silver Ford, MHR entwined in a fancy monogram on the doors. It looked new, powerful, expensive. Obviously the vehicle they must use when going to shows, rodeos, wherever. It reflected more the successful ranching endeavour Amanda suspected Mac ran than his old grey truck.

Smoothing her hair one last time, she grabbed her handbag and a light wrap. Taking a deep breath, just as she did to calm herself before going on stage, Amanda flung open the door.

Both Mac and John-Michael were getting out of the truck. Both were dressed in dark suits. While appreciating how nice they both looked, Amanda was especially conscious of how superbly Mac filled his out. His light shirt threw his tanned face into greater contrast, making him look as dark as an Indian. The lack of his hat was a startling change, his auburn waves gleaming in the late sun. John-Michael remained by the truck as Mac advanced to the steps, studying her, his face impassive.

'Hi.' Amanda smiled brightly. 'Not your usual truck, I see.'

'No, this one's for show. Thought it more appropriate for tonight than the grey one. Glad now I did. You look very ... nice.' His eyes strayed to her lips as he spoke.

Amanda felt the nervousness again, quickly licking her lips. She moved towards the truck, admiring it. Keeping everything on a casual basis.

'Hi, Mandy,' John-Michael easily greeted her. 'Don't think we'll be too crowded, do you?'

'No, it's a big truck. Nice, too.' She slid in as John-Michael held the door. Mac climbed in the driver's side, only inches from Amanda. She sat primly upright. When John-Michael sat down, it was a very close fit. Even more confining as Amanda became more and more aware of Mac's every move. He brushed against her turning to see out of the back window when reversing to the main drive; the contact sent vibrations throughout Amanda's whole body.

Afraid she'd give herself away, she turned to John-Michael.

'Been practising?'

'Not much, I've been busy. I like your hair that way. It's pretty, all fluffy.'

'Thanks.'

Amanda looked out of the windscreen. John-Michael had been her major concern. He was the only one in Timber she knew for certain listened to her records, had an album. If he didn't recognise her, perhaps she exaggerated her fame. Imperceptibly, she relaxed. It was, fortunately, not a long drive.

Elizabeth Burke's house was as stately as its owner. The old Victorian residence, freshly painted, sat in the middle of a manicured lawn, with formal flower-beds flanking the path. A small fence surrounded the garden. There were already two other vehicles drawn up before it when Mac pulled the truck to the kerb.

In only a moment Elizabeth was greeting them at her door, directing John-Michael to take Amanda's wrap; ushering them into her living room. Two other couples were already present, an older man and a much younger, blonde woman on the sofa. Near the fireplace a man and woman were studying a figurine.

'Mac. So good to see you.' The blonde rose swiftly and came to meet him, smiling prettily. 'It's been too long!'

'Sally, may I introduce Amanda Smith to you,' Elizabeth said, intercepting Sally. 'Sally Sutherland. And her father, Henry Sutherland. Henry is Timber's pharmacist,' Elizabeth introduced. Mr Sutherland had followed his daughter to greet the newcomers, though at a more leisurely pace.

'How do you?' Amanda murmured, shaking hands.

The couple by the fireplace turned, friendly smiles of welcome on their faces as they joined the others.

'Ron and Pamela Haversham. This is Amanda Smith, she's a neighbour of Mac's; the singer I was telling you about.'

'How do you do?' Amanda murmured again, smiling at the Havershams. They were a pleasant couple, looking about Mac's age.

'Ron's on the Festival Committee, so you'll see quite a bit of him as the time draws nearer,' Pamela said with a fond look at her husband. 'Have you sung in front of a large audience before?'

'Yes,' Amanda answered briefly.

'You might even find a career in it,' Mac murmured softly, for her ears alone.

Amanda would not rise to the bait. She smiled sunnily up at him. 'Maybe.'

Sally placed a perfectly manicured hand on Mac's arm. 'Come and talk to me. I know you are not the least interested in the festival.'

Amanda glanced at Sally, then back at Mac, a mischievous smile lighting her face. There was a woman on the make if she ever saw one.

'Yes, do go talk with your friend. I'll be fine with my new acquaintances.'

With a hard look at Amanda, as if warning her to watch herself, he went with Sally. They sat on the sofa, Sally plunging immediately into an animated discussion designed to absorb Mac's full attention.

The others remained where they were.

'Elizabeth said you were a a neighbour of Mac's. Are you the one who took Cora's place?' Henry Sutherland asked.

'Yes. I have lots to do with it before it will be the way I envisage it. But I'm very excited about it. It's my first place, you know,' she confided.

'Where are you from?' Pamela asked.

'Most recently, L.A.'

'That explains it,' Ron said. 'Anything would be better than L.A., even a cabin that needed work done to it.'

'Ron, lots of people like L.A.'

'But not Miss Smith, or she'd not be here.'

'Right you are. I already love Timber. But, please, Mandy is my nickname, won't you use that?'

'Glad to. I'm Ron.'

'Henry.'

'Pamela.'

'I'm John-Michael. Is this a new game Aunt

Elizabeth has thought up?' John-Michael joined the group, coming up easily and standing near Amanda.

'No, dear. We are just introducing ourselves again,' Elizabeth said. 'Would you help serve the cocktails? I seem to have lost your father.'

John-Michael glanced at the sofa, smiling at Sally when she waved to him.

'Yes, I guess you did. Sure, I'll help.'

John-Michael took the orders and efficiently matched drinks to the proper individuals. Sally and Mac remained isolated from the others, who moved as a group to sit on the chairs and ottoman between the stone fireplace and long windows overlooking the side garden. Even though they sat apart, Amanda was soon aware of Mac's eyes on her. Twice she looked up, her gaze locking with his, driving all thoughts from her head. Causing her to lose the thread of the conversation around her. After the second incident, she vowed to refrain from looking in his direction, though she was still conscious of his regard, his constant surveillance. It was almost a physical strain to keep her eyes within the group, to refrain from looking at Mac.

'Do you have a job up here?' Pamela asked. 'Are you working?'

'Not right now. I'm sort of taking the summer off,' Amanda replied.

'Are you a teacher?' Henry enquired.

'She's teaching me guitar,' John-Michael volunteered from his perch on the arm of Amanda's chair.

'Wonderful. A good accomplishment to have,' Ron said. 'I think it is good to have a musical outlet, even better to be able to do it yourself.'

'Yes. We enjoy music so, sitting around in the evenings and listening to it. I'm sure it will give you many hours of pleasure, John-Michael,' Pamela said.

'Wait until you hear Mandy sing. You'll love it. Talk

about listening pleasure,' John-Michael said, smiling down at her, his eyes holding hers. 'Everyone who hears her loves it; she is very popular.'

Amanda's eyes widened. He knows who I am! she thought, startled. Then amused. He had never said anything. As she looked questioningly at him, he smiled and nodded slightly. She smiled back at him, closing her right eye in a quick wink.

At least I think he likes me for myself and not for who I am. I wonder how long he has known, she mused, turning back to the others. She would talk to him later!

Amanda was surprised to find, when dinner was announced, that Elizabeth had a maid. Somehow the rugged independence of the rural community had not prepared her for the trappings of the city. Yet, upon closer observation, the maid had probably been with Elizabeth for years; she looked to be the same age. A fitting accompaniment to the stately elegance of the old Victorian house.

The party moved to the formal dining room. A large mahogany table beneath a crystal chandelier dominated the room. It was formally set with fine china, crystal and silver. Mac sat at the head, with Sally and Amanda on either side. Elizabeth was opposite him, with Henry and Ron on her left and right. John-Michael sat opposite Pamela, who was between her husband and Amanda.

The maid served quietly, soup first, then salad and the entrée, fresh mountain trout in a tasty, tangy sauce. The food was delicious. Obviously the maid's talents exceeded the excellent job she did serving.

Conversation lagged while the guests began their meal, the silence a tribute to the excellent cuisine. As the dinner progressed, Amanda was entertained by Sally's rather obvious attempts to monopolise Mac. Observing more than participating, Amanda deduced

Sally would love nothing more than to be the next Mrs John MacKensie. From Mac's scowling expression, Amanda didn't give Sally much of a chance.

Elizabeth's voice broke into the small silence Sally left after an amusing story, swinging Amanda's attention to that end of the table.

'. . . of course, in my younger day, a woman stayed home and tended the household.'

'And so they still should.' Sally jumped in. ' I think being a homemaker is a full-time career in itself. Every woman should strive for that goal.' Sally's eyes slid quickly to Mac, quickly away again.

Elizabeth nodded. 'I agree.'

'If they can and want,' Amanda couldn't resist inserting.

'Huh?' Sally said, rather inelegantly.

'If a woman wants to be a homemaker, fine. It's not always feasible, either economically or emotionally these days,' Amanda said. Seven pairs of eyes stared at her. Open mouth, insert foot, she thought wryly, glancing around the table.

'Well, yes, I can see if someone *had* to work because of money,' Sally reluctantly concurred, 'but, otherwise, I can't understand a woman wanting to go out everyday to a job, competing with men. Her place is in her husband's home, providing for him.'

Amanda wrinkled her nose. 'If I ever get married, I would expect my husband to give me the same respect and support as I would give him. A career that was important to me would, by that mutual respect, also be important to my husband.'

'If you want to work, don't get married,' Sally said.

'Men aren't given that advice,' Amanda said. 'They can have a career, and a home life. They have to help out around the home. Why not a woman doing that, too?'

'I still say a wife's place is in her husband's home. What do you think, Mac?'

'I'm old-fashioned enough to agree. I think it is a fine profession for a woman, taking care of a home, a husband, a family.'

Sally beamed around the table: Mac sided with her!

'Perhaps being at home all the time isn't enough for some people. Look at my mother,' John-Michael interrupted. 'Maybe if she had had something else to do, she wouldn't have run off. I think she was bored.'

From the stunned silence around the table, Amanda realised the taboo he had broken. Her anger rose a little. The poor boy. He probably had always missed his mother, but because of the coddling everyone did to shelter Mac, he was unable to talk about her, resolve any feelings he had, get clarification of what really happened.

'Maybe,' Amanda replied as the others remained awkwardly silent, 'but she was a fool to leave you behind, sweetie.'

John-Michael shot her a grateful glance, then looked apprehensively at his father. Mac's face was closed, his eyes narrowed, going from Amanda to John-Michael and back to Amanda. Sally reached out a consoling hand.

'Maybe she was bored,' Amanda spoke up. 'There isn't much to do keeping a house tidy these days, and with neighbours so far away here in the country, maybe she yearned for something more than she got. I know I would.'

'Well, I've been a full-time homemaker, and worked outside. If you have a job you like, it is rewarding to feel a part of the community. I enjoyed it when I was home all the time, but I had small children that needed me. Once they were grown, it *was* boring to stay home all day alone, no friends close by.' Pam spoke. 'With all the modern appliances we enjoy, the actual work involved in keeping a house is greatly reduced. I like working now. It's not so bad, do you think, Ron?'

'No. I'm happy you're happy, Pamela. Our life together has always been good.'

Amanda smiled at them. Was this another couple like Dave and Evie?'

'I still think a wife's place is in the home,' Sally said.

'And I still think marriage is a partnership, a sharing of two lives, of whatever the two lives are doing, not the abdication of one in total absorption to the other,' Amanda said clearly, meeting and holding Mac's eyes for a long moment, breaking away to look over to Sally. 'Anyway, Sally, it's a useless conversation. I've had these views for years. You probably have had yours for years, too. I know I'm too set to change.' Amanda smiled at the other woman, inviting comment. Almost reluctantly, Sally smiled back.

'You are right, I am too set to change, either.'

'Mandy pans for gold.' John-Michael changed the subject.

The others, eager to lighten the atmosphere, joined in with questions and advice, with an occasional derisive comment thrown in by Mac. Amanda took it all in good part and the rest of the meal passed smoothly.

Coffee was served in the living room. This time everyone sat together, although Sally stayed as close to Mac as she could. The conversation was general and Amanda enjoyed herself, learning more about her new acquaintances while not revealing more about herself than she wished.

When it was time to leave, Amanda and John-Michael were first to the truck, but had to wait for Mac, who had walked Sally to her car. As they sat in the truck and watched them, John-Michael said,

'Sally would like to marry Dad, you know.'

'Do you like her?' Amanda asked. She did know, it was very obvious.

'She's all right. She's been after Dad for years.' He was quiet for a moment. 'I don't think he'll ever marry her, though. He's never even kissed her.'

'You don't know that.' Amanda's face grew warm; she was grateful for the night's cloaking darkness. Mac had kissed her several times. She licked her lips in remembrance. John-Michael only knew of one time. Amanda wouldn't mind if Mac kissed her again. She shook her head; what was she thinking of?

'I know, Mandy,' the boy said definitely.

What could she say to that? There was no need. Mac gave a final wave and moved to join them in the truck. Amanda was achingly aware of Mac when he climbed in. His leg was only inches from hers, his arm almost touching her as he drove the pick-up competently through the blackness, the headlights the only illumination on this moonless night.

Reaching her cabin, he stopped the truck with the lights showing on the steps and front door. Amanda drew her key from her handbag before getting out.

'I'll walk you up,' Mac said.

John-Michael let Amanda out of his door. 'Good night, Mandy,' he said, climbing back in the truck, and turning on the radio while he waited for his father.

'Thank you for taking me.' Amanda reached the front door and unlocked it. Just as the door swung open, the lights of the truck went out, plunging them into total darkness.

'What the hell . . . John-Michael!' Mac turned and roared at his son.

Amanda gave a small giggle. 'He's just being tactful.'

'What does that mean?' Mac's voice lost some of its anger.

She swallowed. 'Only that John-Michael thought we might be more comfortable saying good night in the dark . . .' Amanda trailed off, realising where that might lead.

Mac's hand brushed her cheek, found her shoulders, and drew her slowly up to him.

'He's smarter than I thought,' he said softly, lowering his head to hers.

Amanda thrilled at his touch, revelled in the feel of his fingers as they threaded themselves in her hair, drew themselves through the silken strands. He tilted her head to suit him, thumbs along her jaw bone, as his mouth came down to hers. His lips were warm and persuasive, drawing a willing response from her as she twined her arms around his neck. His tongue moved to invade the softness of her mouth, to tease and tantalise her, causing sensations she had known only once before. In his embrace. Eagerly she returned his pressure, opening her mouth to his assault, losing track of time as the kiss deepened and went on and on.

'I want you, Mandy,' he said harshly against her mouth, his breath mingling with hers.

She felt a small *frisson* of pleasure course through her. 'John-Michael,' she protested.

'I know.' He kissed her again and again, his arms locked around her back, pulling her hard against him. Over and over his mouth took hers, his lips hard and demanding, his tongue filling her senses with a heady feeling of his passion.

'Not tonight, but soon. I mean to have you,' he said, in between kisses. He trailed his lips down her throat, back to her cheek, finding her mouth again.

Amanda could smell the scent of him, of the cologne he was wearing tonight. His hard body against hers was exciting and disturbing. She wanted Mac to keep kissing her, to move his hands as he had the other time. For the moment to go on and on. Forget about John-Michael. Forget about everything, save the feelings Mac could cause. Save Mac.

Finally, reluctantly, slowly, he eased his hold, drew

back. With one last, brief kiss, only lips touching, he turned and left.

The truck reversed and reached the main drive before Mac turned on the headlights, sparing Amanda the harsh glare. She watched the lights disappear through the trees, thoughts churning. Lightly she traced her mouth with her tongue, her lips just slightly swollen from the pressure of his kisses. A smile lifted the corners of her mouth. What a wonderful end to an evening. And there was promise of ... of what?

She had a sudden, dreadful thought. What if Mac thought she went in for casual sex. Just because he thought her a hippie, did he also think she went in for love-ins, and all the other casual relations the hippie image held?

Surely, it wasn't just that?

CHAPTER ELEVEN

THE telephone installation man woke Amanda early the next morning. He was a cheery old man, talked steadily as he wired the cabin from a line he had already strung outside. Amanda liked him, made him coffee and listened to his tales of various customers and the ingenuity it had taken for him to connect some of their remote dwellings with the lines from the local telephone company. Hers, in comparison, was an easy morning's work.

When the man had finished and gone, Amanda used her new phone to call Dave. After giving him her new phone number, she continued, 'Do me a favour and check on the status of my furniture. It was so hectic coming back from Nashville and trying to arrange for them to move my stuff up and still get back up here on the day I said I would, I don't have a definite idea of where it is and when it is due here.'

'I'll check it out right away and let you know,' he promised. 'By the way, I got two new songs from Bob Clive that you might want to hear. I thought they would be good for the new album, if you like them.'

'Sounds promising, what are they like?' Bob Clive was a songwriter whose music Amanda especially enjoyed doing. He had written several of her most successful songs and she was always eager to try his work when he wrote another one for her.

'One's a ballad, the other one is fast, like *Boatman's Shanty Boy*. When can you try them? Shall I send them up to you?'

'Yes, let me see them, then I'll come down for a couple of days after the furniture gets here. I've written another one too. I don't know how you'll like it, though.' The song Dave would probably like, the sentiment was really what she thought he wouldn't like.

'It's probably good; why wouldn't it be? They usually are. I talked to the others about Labor Day. We'll be up in Timber the morning of your festival, full gear and all. It's a noon show, right?'

'No, I think Miss Burke said 2 p.m.; same thing, I guess. You should be here by late morning so we can set up. We can have a picnic, too. How's Evie?'

'Big as a house. She won't make the picnic. I'll let you know when I'm a daddy. Thanks for the number. I'll call you about the furniture when I find out.'

'OK, thanks. Hi to all.'

Amanda hung up slowly. A phone was certainly an added asset to her cabin. Now she could have the best of both words, rural living, yet instant contact with whoever she wanted to talk to regarding business. Perhaps she could work it so plans and transactions could be handled, at least preliminarily, by phone.

Wandering out to the veranda, she drew up a chair, tilted back, feet on the railing. Maybe she'd even get a long lead and conduct business from her veranda! What a set up!

Gazing out at the trees, she thought of what she and Dave had discussed. She did have a new song, but was wondering how he would take the message it gave. Idly, she hummed it through, then again. It was good. She went to get paper, pencil and her guitar. The music had been in her head all summer, the words gradually growing as the days passed. She hummed it again, strumming the guitar.

Time drifted by as she worked on her song. It was almost finished, but she wanted it to be perfect before singing it for the band. She wanted to present it at its best. At one point her pulses quickened when she thought she heard the motor of the big grey pick-up, but nothing came into view and she grinned ruefully. No more wishful thinking; concentrate on the work at hand.

It grew hotter as the sun reached its zenith. Amanda was clad in the usual jeans and a buttoned cotton shirt. Her feet were bare and, as she sat with them on the railing, she considered going inside to change. Shorts would be much more appropriate in the hot afternoon. But first, she'd perfect this last section.

Preoccupied with the composition, Amanda failed to hear the truck when it really did approach, until it was actually turning into her drive.

Throat dry, heart tripping, she stood up, placing her music face down on the table. It might be John-Michael, he drove the truck sometimes. A smile lit her face, however, as Mac climbed out and strode to the veranda.

Amanda moved to meet him. 'Hi, what brings you by?'

'Messenger service,' he replied, skipping stairs, joining her on the veranda, his eyes raking her figure, reminding her of the first time they met. His look did not anger Amanda this time, quite the contrary; she was warmed and excited by it.

'Aunt Elizabeth is having a group meeting next week about the festival. She wants you to come too, if you can. I don't know why she didn't let you know last night, unless they just decided this morning. Anyway, she asked me to come by and let you know.'

'When is it?'

'Next Tuesday, about ten.'

'If I can get there,' she said diffidently.

'If you want a ride, this time you have to ask for it,' he said, staring down at her.

'I do. May I get a lift from you to your aunt's next Tuesday?' she asked sweetly, looking up at the narrowed, gleaming green eyes. He was devastatingly attractive; did he have any idea of the feelings his mere presence caused her? She moved just a little closer, smiling provocatively up to him, flirting almost.

'Yeah, I'll give you a ride.' He watched her as she drew near, a small glint of amusement showing.

'It's hot out here, care for some lemonade? I have some made.'

'Sounds good.'

Amanda moved to enter the cabin, conscious of Mac's closeness, of his following her inside, closing the door to the day's heat. She looked back, caught in his gaze.

Sweeping his hat off, he tossed it on to the table. Extending one arm, he stopped her move to the kitchen, turned her around to face him. Amanda remembered what he had said last night, suddenly felt butterflies in her stomach. She licked her lips, waiting for his next move.

'Mandy,' he said huskily, pulling her close, sheltering her in his embrace.

'Yes?' she whispered as he lowered his head, reaching down to open her mouth with his. Amanda felt a sudden surge of pleasure; she reached up to encircle his neck with her arm, threading her fingers through his thick, wavy hair. It was crisp and smooth as her fingers buried themselves in it. Mac's lips were firm and warm, moving against hers.

His hands pulled her tight against him, moulding her slight frame against the length of him, his mouth claiming all conscious thought from her. Slowly he moved his hand up and down her back, pulling back just a little in surprise.

'Don't you ever wear a bra?' he murmured huskily.

Amanda smiled and moved closer. 'Not when I'm relaxing alone at home.'

'But you're not alone now.'

'Nor very relaxed,' she murmured back as he claimed her mouth again, one hand slipping beneath the back of her loose-fitting shirt, his fingers warm against her soft smooth skin. As he explored her back, she shivered with delight and anticipation, a strong feeling of desire growing within her with the feather light caresses he made against her skin with his hand, his other hand holding her head firmly for his kisses.

She revelled in them, responded to his kisses, tracing his mouth with her tongue, meeting his thrust with her own, scarcely aware of anything but Mac's mouth on hers and his hands on her body.

He raised his head and glanced around. 'Why don't you have a sofa like everyone else, so we could sit down?' he growled, his voice low.

'Cushions are fine.' Amanda led him over, trailing her hands down his arms as she lowered herself to one of the large soft cushions near the wall. Mac, beside her, drew her up against him, his touch thrilling, exciting. On and on the kiss went, slowly warming Amanda, slowly awakening vague desires and longings. Mac pulled back, looking into her eyes, holding them as he slowly reached out to unbutton her shirt, his fingers brushing against her bare skin as he fumbled with the unfamiliar task.

Amanda trembled slightly, could feel her insides begin to melt when he opened her shirt, reaching again for her. His mouth claimed hers as his fingers gently traced the curves and valleys of her body. She moved to draw closer to him, but he held her off a little, his hand wandering down her breast, across to the other, back to her throat. Down again. She moved beneath his hands, caught in the sensations and longings Mac drew from her. He moved to the fastener of her jeans. She caught her breath as he eased down the zipper.

Slowly Amanda unbuttoned his checked shirt, moving then to embrace him, her bare breasts pressing warmly against his chest. Mac drew her in his arms and slowly pulled her back on top of him as he lay against the cushions.

The feel of Mac's skin beneath her fingers, his mouth evoking wonderful sensations, caused time to stand still, her head to spin. She wanted him. When he gently rubbed his knuckles down her ribs, near her breasts, she gave a sigh of pure happiness. Soon, soon she would be complete. This yearning, this desire growing within her would be assuaged. She began to tremble a little when he rolled her on her back. She wasn't *afraid*, just unsure exactly what to expect.

'Oh, Mandy, girl. You're so soft and pretty,' Mac whispered against her ear as his mouth feathered kisses along her cheek, to her throat, down her neck.

She smiled dreamily at his words, eager for his mouth to return to hers.

The shrill, strident ring of the telephone shattered the afternoon stillness.

'What the hell is that?' Mac growled, startled. He pulled away abruptly.

'My phone. I just got it today.' She sat up. 'I guess I should answer it.'

'Yes, I guess you should. Did you have to get the model with the loudest ring?'

Amanda smiled and lithely rose, moving quickly into the kitchen. The ring was harsh in the drowsy afternoon. Could she adjust the loudness?

'Hallo?'

'Hi, Mandy, Dave here.'

'Hi.'

'Your furniture left a few days ago. Should arrive in Timber later this week. They have your address, and directions, but don't know you have a phone, so don't wander off or they might dump everything in the front yard.'

'I'll stay close. Thanks for checking for me, Dave.'

'No problem. I'll talk to you soon.'

Amanda replaced the receiver and turned, eager to rejoin Mac. He was standing in the doorway, an inscrutable expression on his face. Gone was the tender look she had seen in his eyes only moments ago. He had already re-buttoned his shirt and tucked it back into his jeans.

'Do yourself up. Someone's coming.'

Amanda's eyes widened. She quickly moved to refasten her jeans and shirt. She could hear the gravel in the driveway crunching. Who was it? John-Michael? She moved to see. Mac remained squarely in the doorway, blocking her way.

'Another time, hmm, Mandy?' he said gently, reaching down to lightly brush against her lips.

'I hope so,' she said frankly, essaying a small smile against her disappointment. It had been a heady time; still the phone had been a lifesaver if she was really having another visitor now.

A soft knock.

Amanda opened the door to Elizabeth Burke.

'Good afternoon, Amanda. How are you?'

'Hi, Miss Burke, come on in. Your nephew is here.'

'I know, I saw the truck. Hi, Mac.'

'Aunt Elizabeth. Did you worry I wouldn't pass on your invitation.?'

'Don't be silly, dear boy.'

Amanda hid a smile, darting a quick glance at the 'dear boy'. A less likely looking boy Amanda couldn't imagine.

'No, I decided to discuss part of the programme for the festival with Amanda prior to the meeting.'

'That's my cue to leave, then. I'll see you Mandy. Tuesday, if not before.'

'Thank you. And . . . thanks for stopping by today.'

'My pleasure.' His eyes on her mouth.

.She licked her lips as he passed to leave,

disappointment flooding through her. It had been wonderful; she was sorry he was leaving.

Elizabeth Burke sat primly on one of the dining chairs, nodding to her nephew as he left.

'I did want to get this cleared up, my dear. I hope I'm not coming at an inopportune time.'

'Not at all. Would you like some lemonade?' She remembered asking Mac the same thing only a short time ago.

'Not today, thank you, Now, did your group agree to come, too, to sing in the festival?'

'Yes, they will arrive that morning. I think I heard you say the entertainment wouldn't start until after noon. Is that right?'

'Yes, around 2 p.m. usually. That gives everyone time to eat and be finished so they can then devote full attention to the performance. After the show, there are games, then a barbecue and fireworks after dark. A local high school group will play music at dusk for those who want to dance. We try for a professional group or troupe for the main feature. I do hope you will be able to handle it.'

Elizabeth frowned and added fretfully, 'I do wish Mac would come, or at least permit John-Michael to attend. They both miss such good events each year.' She shook her head. 'Well it can't be helped. Now, we need about an hour's entertainment; is that too long?'

Amanda smiled. 'No problem. We have played large audiences before and usually do fine. I sing country songs, did you know that?'

'Oh, my dear, that will be splendid! It's very popular in Timber. The rock music doesn't seem too much in demand these days, except for some of the teenagers. Now, if you need anything, loudspeakers, costumes, whatever, do make a list for the committee. We can get things like that.'

Briefly Amanda thought of their travelling bus

loaded with a dozen or more costume changes and thousands of dollars worth of electrical equipment.

'We have all we need,' she replied. 'We'll just need access to a power source.'

'Of course. A large audience won't worry you?'

'No, we have played before large groups before.' Audiences larger than the entire town of Timber.

Elizabeth nodded, satisfied. 'Well, I guess that covers it. If you do want to set up your equipment early, the stage should be finished by ten or so. It's portable, you know, and we erect it each year for the festival.' She rose. 'I look forward to our meeting on Tuesday. You'll have a chance to meet the others working on the festival and we will get an overview of the entire set of activities so we can see how the day will go.'

'I look forward to it, too. I'll see you next week.'

As Elizabeth backed her car out, Amanda again marvelled at the way the entertainment was set for such an important event in the little town's social calendar. No audition, no contract, just a fond great-aunt's acceptance of a high-school boy's evaluation of a new neighbour. How did they know she really could sing? That she was any good? That she could be counted on? It certainly was a different way of handling a gig than most she experienced.

Turning from the door when Miss Burke left, Amanda's eyes alighted on the cushions, now stacked neatly against the wall. How far would things have gone had the phone not rung, Elizabeth not come by? Amanda questioned if she would have drawn back, or not? She hugged herself with loneliness, wishing Mac were still here.

Mac sounded the horn Tuesday morning. It was not necessary; Amanda had been watching for him for over half an hour. She opened her door even as the horn was still echoing, running lightly down the stairs and climbing into the truck. Her hair was again pulled back, the tinted glasses in place. Her jeans were new and still dark blue, the cotton top informal but not too casual.

'Good morning,' she said brightly. She gave him a warm smile, not letting the disappointment she had felt the last few days show. She had not seen nor spoken to Mac since he left after Elizabeth's unexpected arrival. She had waited each day, but nothing from Mac MacKensie.

'Morning,' he replied, setting the truck in motion. He did not speak again and the ride continued in silence. Mac finally broke it only when Elizabeth's home came into view.

'I'll pick you up in a couple of hours. That should be enough time.'

'OK. Thanks.' Amanda got out as soon as he had stopped the truck, slamming the door and going to the house without a backward glance. Blow hot, blow cold. What made the man tick? She was upset he continued to be so difficult to get to know. And she wanted to so much.

Elizabeth Burke had the meeting well organised. All points she wanted covered were listed out and she was firm in keeping the discussion firmly on one point at a time. The concessions committee reported its area under control, with plenty of Cokes, beer, hot dogs, hamburgers and chips being brought in for the townsfolk who didn't want to bring their own food to the festivities. Ron Haversham was in charge of games. He reported them well in hand: horsehoe set-ups would be ready by ten; volley-ball nets up then as well. Softball was scheduled for after the singing event.

Amanda reported that she had a back-up band that would be coming up for the festival and would be bringing their own equipment. She gave a list of songs she thought she would sing, leaving several slots open to be filled that day with songs that were her special trademark. No sense, if they didn't require it, in letting them all know now who she was. Time enough later. But she felt more confident now and, if the exposure came early, it wouldn't matter so much. There was mild speculation about the band but, when the crafts committee spoke, the interest faded. A large number of townspeople were bringing handicrafts to sell at the festival and booths would be set up early to catch the first arrivals.

Elizabeth distributed a list of participants, schedule of events and contact phone numbers. Everyone dutifully added Amanda's number when she informed them she now had a phone.

'The festival should be a resounding success this year, and we can all be proud of our contributions.' Elizabeth closed the meeting. 'I will be in touch with each of you as the need arises, but see no call for another joint meeting.'

Amanda looked for a clock. They had been less than the two hours Mac had estimated. Not that it mattered, she could easily wait out front, it was a pleasant day. When she left with the rest of the committee, however, she was surprised to see the grey truck parked across the road, in the shade.

Though her heart gave a leap of delight to see him, Amanda tried to school her features to remain as impassive as Mac's. With a small shock, Amanda realised she loved this bitter, disapproving man. She wanted to spend time with him, bring a little happiness to him if he would let her. To show him that another one cared for him, for his well being, and happiness. To share her time with him. With a rush of affection, she saw he was watching her cross the road, his eyes following her, his manner and actions speaking louder to her than his words ever had. She smiled as she climbed into the pick-up.

'Meeting done?' he asked, starting the engine.

'Sure is, the festival plans are in full swing now. It sounds like fun. According to Elizabeth, *everyone* will be there.' Amanda looked at him as he kept his eyes on the road. 'Are you and John-Michael coming to it? Can I have a ride?'

Mac shot her a quick look, deep lines of disapproval etched in his face.

'We don't go.'

'Why not?' Dangerous ground.

'We don't go to the festival.'

'Well, come this year. I won't always be at them, this may be my only time. You can hear me sing.'

Amanda noticed how his hands tightened on the wheel, till the knuckles were white. His jaw was clenched, his mouth tight.

She sighed and turned to look out the window. Were the memories still so painful for him? Could he not let the past go? What chance would she ever have against the errant Liza MacKensie?

As the driveway drew near, Mac seemed to relax a little. 'Want to come up for lunch?' he asked.

Surprised, Amanda agreed.

'It is so incredibly beautiful up here,' she said when they reached Mac's place. 'There is a sense of peace and serenity you don't find in many places.'

'I know.' He looked at her a long moment, then led the way into the house.

'Come into the kitchen.' He walked through, Amanda following.

The modern kitchen was surrounded by large windows giving access to the view. The far end of the room was the dining area, with large, sliding glass doors leading to the veranda.

Amanda kept silent, afraid if she said more about the view he would think she was gushing.

'Roast beef OK?'

Mac was drawing things from the refrigerator.

'Fine.' She moved to stand by him, helping a little as they made the sandwiches; he got the soft drinks.

They ate at the table, talking desultorily at first. When hunger had been satisfied, Amanda asked him about the town of Timber, how it came to be, how long his family had been residents. Moving on to other topics, like her life in Colorado.

They skirted some issues, Mac's marriage, Amanda's career. Yet she still felt they were communicating, were drawing closer, or was it only wishful thinking on her part? Perhaps one day soon they could trust each other enough to discuss even the delicate issue they avoided this day.

Amanda realised they were spending the greater part of the afternoon still at the table, that Mac probably had work to attend to, but she wasn't going to bring it up and end the pleasant exchange. It wasn't often they could meet and talk, without setting off sparks.

The conversation veered to her cabin, Amanda mentioning that her furniture had arrived and she would be painting the walls to spruce up the place some more.

'It will be a big job, though, so I'm putting it off a little,' she smiled.

'I had this house repainted a year or so ago. It is a big job, but all places need it every so often.'

'Yes, I guess. I haven't seen all of your house. May I?' Amanda asked. The living room she had seen, now the kitchen. She knew John-Michael's bedroom was off the living room, but the rest?

'Sure. This is the kitchen.' Mac rose and led the way back into the living room. Opening John-Michael's door, he stood aside so Amanda could see the room. John-Michael had posters over most of the walls: singing stars, the Incredible Hulk, one of Evel Knievel's daring jumps. It was remarkably tidy for a teenager's room, she thought.

Back towards the kitchen Mac opened a door leading to a small hallway. Amanda preceded him, pausing at one door.

'Bathroom.' Mac opened it for her to examine. Moving down the hall he opened another door. 'Guest room.'

Across the hall from that one was another door; opening it, he let her glimpse the office. 'I have a larger office, with all the stud records and all down near the main barn; this is more for household accounts and the like.'

He passed the next door, heading straight for the one at the end of the hall, but she stopped by it.

'What's in here?'

He turned, paused and slowly came back up to her, opening the door.

'It was the nursery. John-Michael used it until he was older, and moved to the room he currently has.'

It was dusty and dark, the furniture that a baby would use. It was a sad, neglected room, reflecting all the hopes gone wrong from a marriage. Amanda was sorry she had asked to see it.

'One more and we're done.' Mac pulled the door shut and continued to the end of the hall.

The last door opened to reveal the master bedroom. Again, sliding glass doors opened on to the veranda, framing the mountains in a living mural. A large bed dominated the room, rich brown coverlet reaching the floor. A triple dressing-table and tall wardrobe filled one wall, yet were not too much for the room's size. A dressing room and bathroom led off from the back.

Amanda's heart began thudding in her chest. This was Mac's room. Where he slept at night, got dressed each day. She looked around, taking in all the details, storing them in her memory for the future. She would be able to envisage him here when she was on tour, when she was away from Timber. Moving further into the room, she looked out the window to learn the view he saw first thing each morning.

The door clicked shut.

Spinning round, Amanda found Mac close to her, disturbingly close.

'It's a nice place,' she said huskily, mesmerised by his gaze.

Without reply he reached out and slowly drew her into his arms, as if giving her time to pull away, should she so desire.

To pull away was the last thing she wanted. When his lips touched her, Amanda relinquished all pretence. This was where she longed to be, in the arms of the man she loved. She pressed closer, opening her mouth against his insistent pressure, delighting in the feelings and sensations he caused in her. A thrill of pleasure ran through her as his hands caressed her, as his mouth evoked desire in her down to her toes. When she felt his hands on the bare skin of her back, she thought she would fall down if he didn't hold her up, so weak were her knees. His hands were warm and caressing, rubbing her from her waist to her neck, down again, round to the sides, rubbing his knuckles gently against her ribs. He trailed his mouth down her neck, kissing the soft hollow at the base of her throat, running his hands lightly over her breasts, finding and releasing the bra fastening, moving to caress her, fondle her, all the while pressing warm kisses against her pulsating skin. Amanda was delirious with delight, swept along on the rising flow of sensations Mac was creating within her. She clung to him shamelessly, returning his kisses, unbuttoning his shirt to feel the ripple of muscles along his chest, his shoulders. A feeling of intimacy spread as she ran her fingers over his shoulders, up to his neck to thread through his thick hair.

Shrugging out of his shirt, Mac drew Amanda's top from her, letting his eyes wander over her firm figure before drawing her against him again.

'Oh, Mandy, girl. I've such a hunger for you,' he ground out.

Amanda thought her heart would burst with happiness. 'I for you,' she whispered back.

Almost without her realising it, they moved to the large bed, lying across the soft brown cover. Slowly and deliberately Mac drew his hands across her body, leaving trails of quivering flesh as Amanda arched closer, revelling in his touch, in the responses he was drawing from her.

His hands undid her zip, moving to caress the soft skin of her belly, roving the length of her to her throat, then back down again.

Amanda was aching with desire. She knew there must be more, must be a completion of the longings he had aroused; how to find it?

'Mandy.' Mac continued moving his hand gently over her curves, lifting his head a little.

She opened her eyes to meet his gaze. Mac was no longer so disapproving, but looked under a strain.

'What?' she replied, moving beneath his touch.

'I didn't mean for this to happen, you know,' he replied, his hands continuing their quest.

She licked her lips; it was hard to concentrate on what he was saying; she wanted to lose herself in his touch.

'What?' she repeated.

He gave her a quick kiss. 'This; me and you. Will you marry me, Mandy?'

CHAPTER TWELVE

Her eyes flew open in shocked surprise. Rolling away from him, she sat up on the bed, staring at him.

'Do you mean it? Marriage?'

He lay back against his pillows and watched her. 'Yes, of course I mean it. Do you think I go round asking everyone I meet?'

'No, but I thought you didn't even like me. That you wanted me to move on.'

'Well, I did at first. I disapprove of your lifestyle, your choice of friends. We fight almost every time we get together, but I still keep thinking of reasons to seek you out, of getting us together again. This last week has been the longest I have ever spent. I felt sick earlier when you said this festival may be the only one you go to. You could move on. I've been fighting a losing battle ever since that kiss by the creek.'

She gave a soft gurgle of laughter, remembering the pan of water she had thrown at him. Then her face softened. A dream come true. The man she loved loved her and wanted to marry her. She paused; she thought he loved her, but he hadn't said so in words.

She opened her mouth to ask, but was forestalled.

'Don't answer right away, unless you can say yes. I've been thinking long and hard on it, especially since last week.' He reached out and caught her, pulling her up to him. 'I can't think when you're sitting like that,' he growled softly in her ear. She moved to cuddle closer, fascinated by what he had to say.

'We don't know each other very well,' she began, 'and don't agree on basic issues, like a wife working . . .'

Amanda said, hugging him closer to her, wanting all doubts swept away.

'I know we don't, but I have been thinking a lot this past week or so. Perhaps there is something to a woman working outside the house. The modern conveniences we enjoy all around don't make keeping a home very challenging. If you feel so strongly that you want to work, then I will gladly share your life with your job.'

She looked up, now would be the time to tell him what she did, why it would be more than sharing just a job with someone who left each morning and came home that night. There would be weeks on the road, quick trips to Nashville, to Los Angeles.

He shook his head. 'No, let me finish. As to knowing each other, I only have fifty or so years I can set aside to get to know you. Won't that be enough?

'We have a similar feeling for the countryside round here. You're kind to children, witness John-Michael and his guitar lessons. You are exciting to me, not the usual woman I've met in later years. I want to spend as much of my time with you as I can.'

'Fifty years might be long enough. I should like to marry you, Mac.' She reached up to kiss him.

He rolled her on her back, as the kiss deepened and intensified. Flames of desire rose in Amanda as her arms pulled Mac tighter against her. When his hands moved to her jeans, he whispered against her throat.

'My life was torn apart once by the festival; maybe this year it will put it back together.'

'I hope so. Oh, Mac, love me.' Amanda reached her arms around his neck, giving herself up to his embrace. There was so much to discuss, to clarify; her career, his first marriage. But now, there was only Mac and her and their love.

'Dad?' John-Michael's voice could be heard from a distance. Mac went suddenly still.

'Dad?' John-Michael was closer.

'Dammit, what does it take?' Mac asked, rolling over and moving swiftly to the door. 'Phones, aunts, kids. What next?' He reached the door and opened it just a crack.

'Hi, Dad. Ted and I fixed that stretch of fence.' John-Michael was right on the other side.

Frowning with frustration, Amanda got up and retrieved her top, slipping it quickly on. She stuffed her bra in her jeans pocket and smoothed back her hair. She went to stand by the window while Mac talked to his son. The mood was changed, she doubted they would resume where they had left off. Still, her heart sang! She was engaged to marry John MacKensie. A smile of sheer happiness spread across her face as her spirits soared. Who would have thought the bus ride to Timber would end so happily? She would be with him all the time, when she wasn't on tour.

Oh, God! What would Mac say when she told him what she did for a living? That the job he would be sharing her with involved weeks when she would be away from home, travelling, leading a totally different life from the one in Timber. He knew nothing about her current life. With his temper, he'd explode when she told him. He thought he knew all that was important: she was a hippie, from Colorado. He was adamant against deceit of any kind. He'd be so angry.

Well, she would just wait a little longer. Until he was in a good, loving mood again, not now. For the time being, she would savour this moment. Savour the love she felt for him. Her own, darling, disapproving Mac.

'No.' Mac sounded exasperated. Amanda turned to watch him, love evident in her face, in her eyes as she moved to be near him. Mac ran a hand through his hair, still blocking the door.

'No, what?' Amanda asked.

'That's torn it.' He turned and went for his shirt. John-Michael slowly pushed open the door, grinning when he saw Amanda standing in his dad's room.

'Hi, Mandy.'

'Hi, yourself, John-Michael.' She tried to maintain her composure in the face of this kid with the knowing grin.

'Come on, Mandy, I'll take you home.' Mac was dressed. He reached for her hand, leading her out. As he passed by John-Michael he stopped, glinted down on the boy.

'Mandy's going to marry me,' he said, watching the expressions chase across his son's face, from incredulity to disbelief to delight.

'Hey, that's great!'

'I'll be back later.' Mac led the way to the truck, throwing Amanda a friendly smile as they climbed in.

She was warmed by his look and smiled back, feeling as if she were floating on air. She still couldn't believe it.

'You coming in?' she asked when they reached the cabin.

'Damn right, I am. We were interrupted.'

She laughed. 'Again.'

Climbing out of the truck, she heard her phone ringing. 'I'll run and get it.'

Probably whoever was calling would hang up before she could reach it, but she would try. Made it.

'Mandy? Mandy, this is Dave. Evie fell. She's in the hospital and ... God, Mandy, she's not doing well. Can you come? I need you, coz, they ... they don't know if Evie will make it.'

Amanda closed her eyes against the pain in his voice. Her dear cousin; what an awful thing to happen. They were so happy, and so looking forward to their baby.

'Of course I'll come, Davie. Right away. The baby?'

'They don't know. They don't know if the baby will live or if,' he voice broke a little, 'if Evie will either. Mandy, what will I do if Evie dies?'

'I'll be there as soon as I can get there. Are you at home, or at the hospital?'

'I'm at the hospital, it's St Paul's. I can't see her just yet. What will I do without Evie? What will I do if she doesn't make it?'

'She will, she will. Hold on Davie. I'll be there as soon as I can make it. Hang in.'

Amanda put down the receiver, tears swimming in her eyes. She turned. Mac was blocking the door, his face impassive.

'Oh, Mac, I've got to go. I've got to get home. Can you take me ...' Where? She wanted to get to an airport, a plane would be the fastest way to get to Los Angeles. Even at that it would take hours.

'Where's the nearest airport? Maybe I can get a flight to L.A. My cousin's has a bad fall. She ...' Amanda dashed away the tears, finding herself in Mac's warm arms.

'Easy, girl, we'll get you to an airport. Stockton's only an hour or so away. I'll call for reservations then we'll go. You go pack something while I call.'

'Thanks, Mac.' She drew strength from him, gave him a last hug then hurried to throw a few things in her shoulder bag. She still had lots of things in her L.A. apartment; clothes were the last of her worries right now.

'Ready.' She came out to the living room.

Her furniture was in and arranged nicely, totally changing the outlook of the cabin. There was even a sofa, as Mac had once wanted. They didn't even have a chance to comment on it.

'Let's go. I booked you on the 6 p.m. flight, it's the last direct one out. We'll make it.'

The drive down was a blur to Amanda. She was worried about her cousin, and about Evie. Dave had always been so strong. To have him so distraught was frightening. She prayed Evie at least would be spared. What had happened? From where had she fallen to be so gravely injured. Please let Evie be all right, for Dave's sake. Please.

'I won't waste time trying to park, just drop you off. We're cutting it close, but you'll make it,' Mac said as they took the airport exit from Highway 99.

Amanda hadn't realised they were so near. Her mind was whirling, she could not concentrate on anything but getting to Evie and Dave.

'Fine, that will be OK.' She gathered her things as he pulled up before the airline door.

She looked at him. 'Thank you, Mac.'

He kissed her lightly, his eyes very sombre. 'Come back, Mandy.'

'Of course.' She got out and hurried into the airport.

From Stockton to Los Angeles is not a long flight, less than an hour and a half. To Amanda it seemed endless. Her thoughts were in turmoil. Scarcely believing the misfortune that had befallen Dave, she tried to imagine what had happened, how Evie could have fallen, and so seriously. She was scared, wished she could have had Mac beside her.

Mac. How quickly their special moment had ended. How different things might be had John-Michael not come home early. Though she could not have reached Los Angeles today had she not heard the news when she did, she did wistfully wish she could have remained in ignorance for just a little longer; had had just a little time with Mac and their new-found love. A night of inactivity, or worry and long-distance concern would have been worse, she supposed. Her heart ached for Dave. How devastated she would be if anything happened to Mac. And she and he had not yet had time together to grow closer, to develop into an interdependent partnership, to forge a life together. How much more Dave must be feeling.

Hurry, she urged the jetliner, hurry, hurry.

By the time Amanda reached St Paul's Hospital she was calm, her emotions firmly under control. What would be, would be. She'd wait to hear further when she did.

She found her cousin, with Sam and Phil, in the intensive care reception area. Dave's face lightened when he saw her and he strode across the tiled floor to hug her in a tight embrace.

'How's Evie?' she asked immediately.

His reply was shaky. 'Holding on. They delivered the baby, Caesarean-section. It's a girl. Evie wanted a girl.'

'I know, and you want what Evie wants.' They moved to join the others.

'Hi, guys.'

'Mandy.'

'Hi, sugar. Bad scene, isn't it?' Sam gave her a hug.

'I'll say. When will they know more?' she asked.

Sam shrugged, looked at Dave, then replied, 'Seems the longer she holds on, the better her chances are. They just don't know.'

'What happened?'

Dave told her of Evie's fall down the concrete stairs leading from a friend's second floor apartment. She had hit her head severely and it was that trauma which was life threatening.

'And the baby? Have you seen her? What's her name?'

Dave shook his head. 'She's in guarded condition, whatever that means. Hasn't had a very good birthday.'

The hours stretched out as they talked softly,

comforted each other and waited. Waited for some word from the doctors.

It was close to midnight when a weary resident came to tell them to go home. They did not anticipate any change before morning, if then, but would call instantly if there were any. The hospital was going on its night shift, usually the quietest time at St Paul's. They would all be better rested the next day if they got a good night's sleep tonight.

Dave was finally convinced, and Amanda went home with him. They would all be back in the morning.

The days dragged by. Evie's condition stabilised a little, but she remained in a coma. The baby, in spite of her shaky beginning, was soon thriving. When she was discharged from the hospital at the end of a week, Amanda took charge of her, calling her Davie's Baby. Dave refused to name the child, claiming that it was Evie's choice. He would wait for Evie.

The entire band was back in Los Angeles by this time, rallying around, taking turns sitting with Dave at Evie's bedside, or helping Amanda with the baby.

As the days passed, Amanda gradually assumed some of the managerial roles Dave usually performed. The second week she was there, she suggested they begin rehearsals again for the forthcoming album. She tried the new songs from Bob Clive, and immediately decided to include them. Her two songs from early in the summer were already on the list. She introduced the one she had just finished. The others approved, both of the song and the sentiments it expressed. Explanations were shared and congratulations given. Now if only Dave approved.

Twice Amanda called Mac, but he was very distant and unresponsive the first time, and out when she called again. She spoke at length to John-Michael, leaving her number and telling him what was going on. And, that it looked like her trip to the south of the state would last longer than she had thought.

She got Elizabeth Burke's number from John-Michael, and called to reassure that they would be there in plenty of time for the festival, but might not come prior to the day itself. Amanda didn't want the older woman to become concerned because of Amanda's lengthy absence.

The days were full, the nights dragged. Uncertainties and doubts arose as she lay awake long into the night. Mac had never said he loved her. Could he be so obsessed with acquiring the land that he'd resort to marriage? She did not think so. He had dropped that topic once she had given him the option agreement. She thought he cared for her, did want her. She must be important for him to propose marriage. An affair would be less permanent from his viewpoint but he had not suggested that. Then, why not call her? Why the long silence on his part? Maybe he didn't like the telephone, but surely he'd want to make some contact with her. Maybe if she gave him her address, he'd write. That seemed even less likely. Somehow Amanda didn't see him with a pen in hand; he belonged more to the outdoors. Maybe he was regretting his hasty proposal, maybe he had had second thoughts. Amanda didn't know what to think. She only knew she ached all over with loneliness and longing.

As Amanda was bathing Davie's Baby one morning, the phone rang. A jubilant Dave was calling to tell her Evie was conscious, aware, and the doctors gave their prognosis of a full recovery.

All the members of the troupe were overjoyed and relieved with the news. Life again became pleasurable. Activity picked up, preparing the bus for the trip to Timber and the autumn concert tour, testing all the equipment, last-minute rehearsals, Dave joining in at last. Plans and confirmations of reservations were handled for the autumn tour, everything was falling into place.

The days became more and more hectic as loose ends were wrapped up, as life geared up again for a concert tour of over thirty performances. The idyllic getaway summer was over. Evie was home, Dave back with the band, the baby named, and the world right again.

Amanda tried again to call Mac, but only talked with John-Michael.

'Tell your father I'll be there Labor Day for the festival. For sure. You're going this year, aren't you?'

'Yes, for the first time. Shall we meet you before you sing?'

'Heavens, yes. We'll be there about ten, I hope. You and your Dad should be able to get there around then too. I don't have to do much with the setting up. The guys do that part.'

'Are you coming by bus?'

'Yes, my own this time,' she said carelessly. 'We'll drive straight to the fairground.'

'We'll see you about ten, then, *Amanda*,' John-Michael replied. She had still not talked to John-Michael to see how he knew who she was. There would be time. When she got to Timber.

'Good. Tell your father . . .' There was so much she wanted to say. But not through a third person. 'Tell him I said hi.'

CHAPTER THIRTEEN

THE next stop would be the fairground in Timber! Amanda and the men in her band had driven up from Los Angeles in the big black and silver bus, 'Amanda' emblazoned on its side. After a night's stop-over in Stockton, the bus was on the last leg of the journey to Timber. They would arrive right on time for setting up for the performance at the festival. Sam was at the wheel, making the curvy mountain hills seem like park driving as he babied the bus around bends, coaxed it up the hills, coasted down.

Amanda was impatient to reach their goal. She couldn't wait to see Mac. They still had a lot to discuss, decisions and plans to make. All that notwithstanding, she was just plain dying to see him again, be with him. While glad she had been able to help her cousin, she still felt a little short-changed for her own summer, her own engagement, the only one she would have.

Only this one engagement. She planned to stay married to one man for life, believing in the old until-death-do-us-part words. She was not a green young girl, infatuated by love's first breath, but a mature woman, sure in herself, confident in the love she felt for Mac MacKensie. Still, it would have been nice to have had a normal engagement. She didn't even know when he wanted to get married! There had been no long walks together, just the two of them; no intimate dinners; no time to really get to know each other. She smiled, remembering he had said he only had fifty years left. Would it be enough? She doubted it.

Hurry, she urged the bus, just as she had once

urged a big jet. This time it was for herself. Hurry.
Hurry.

As they drew near, drew close to the river called
Mokelumne, Amanda sat on the edge of her seat. It
was with growing pleasure she recognised landmarks
now. Soon, very soon, they'd be there.

Yes, here was the bridge. Soon they'd turn left, take
that road to the fairground. She was sure of the
directions, Miss Burke had been specific. There, that's
where it was. Hurry.

Sam pulled the big bus into the gravel parking area
by the fairground, swinging wide around the cars
already parked, slowing for the pedestrians in the lot.
Amanda was surprised at the number of people there,
already working getting things ready. Already visiting
with friends and neighbours. The concession stands
were being erected; tables and tents for the arts and
crafts section being set up. In the distance, volley-ball
nets were being strung; iron stakes pounded in for
horseshoes.

Sam skilfully manoeuvered the big bus close to the
portable stage erected on the grass at the far end of the
field, near the parking lot. As the bus lumbered along,
crunching gravel, spurting dust from beneath its
wheels, heads turned, speculation ran riot. Several
people wandered near the vehicle, then a few more.
When Sam finally stopped and opened the door, one
bold teenager approached.

'Is this for Amanda, the country singer?'

'Sure is, miss,' he answered cheerfully, giving her a
big grin as he climbed down the bus.

'*Riverboat Gambler* Amanda?' called another.

Sam smiled and nodded.

'Oh, wow!'

The word began to spread.

Dave, Joe and the others quickly joined Sam and
fell into their routine, to set up as they did for all the

shows, unloading equipment, putting it in place on the stage. Stringing electric cable, connectors. Testing the instruments, the amplifiers. More and more people were drawn to watch, some to stake claims to good seats, others to speculate with friends as they kept a watchful eye on the activities.

Amanda hung back, remained in the bus. She was not usually a part of this. Her job came later, during the show. For now she was free to stay in the bus, her eyes searching the parking lot for a beat-up old grey pick-up truck. She fairly seethed with impatience. Where was he?

Her hair was clean, shiny and newly trimmed. It waved and curled around her face, framing it softly, catching highlights in the sun. She wore a silver outfit, fringed and embroidered, remembering he had said the colour would suit her. Her make-up was on, she was ready. Where was Mac? It was after ten. Where was he?

She saw the truck, just turning into the parking lot, driving slowly towards the bus. Her heart lodged in her throat. Mac. She scrambled from the bus, eager to meet him. She had missed him so!

'Amanda, can I have your autograph?' One girl, leaning against the bus, thrust a paper and pencil in her face. 'I'm so excited to meet you. I can't wait to hear you sing. I didn't know you were the main attraction. Boy, am I glad I came to the festival this year.'

'Can I have your autograph, too?' another asked.

'Me, too?' still another clamoured.

There were a dozen or more young people surrounding her, exclaiming their happiness at her being at the festival, smiling shyly at the famous star in their midst. Eager to gain her attention, to obtain the personal favour of an autograph. And impeding her progress.

Smiling, Amanda signed each request, impatience seething within her, outwardly serene and at ease with the group, answering questions, writing what was asked of her. She was where she was in the industry today because of her fans. She would be gracious, and patient and smiling and . . .

There, the last one signed. With a smile all round, she moved eagerly to the pick-up.

A feeling of *déjà vu*. Mac leaning against the side, arms crossed, face angered. Amanda's heart sank. She didn't blame him for being angry, there was a lot she had never told him. What a way for him to find it out, too, just arrive and be slapped in the face with the big bus, the crowds, all the things he had never suspected about her. She wished more than ever that she had told him of her career, or why she was spending the summer incognito. Their time had been cut short.

He hated deceit, he had been very clear about that the day of the picnic in the big clearing. She would have to give a good presentation of why she had not told him initially who she was, what she did. But later. Now she was so very glad to see him; wasn't he glad to see her?

'Hi, Mac.' She stopped close to him, tilting her head back to smile so happily up at him, shocked at the glittering green eyes, the lines of disapproval and anger deep set.

'The famous *Amanda* deigned to visit the mountain yokels one more time. A triumphant return, I might add.'

'I can explain . . .' she began. Oh, oh, it looks like explanations must come now, not later.

'Save your lies *Amanda*. I have been fooled before and God help me it looks as if I have been again.'

'No.'

Mac stood up, towering above her, anger emanating from every inch of him. 'What a fun summer, have a

fling with a yokel, then high-tail it back to Los
Angeles and your lover there when things start turning
serious here. Well, serious is off, now. You've had
your fun and I've had mine. I should have taken more
when I had the chance, but we're even now, and
quits!'

'No, Mac, please listen.' Amanda was scared. She
put a tentative hand on his arm. Had she ruined
everything by her desire for secrecy, by her wish to be
just plain Mandy Smith for a summer? No, he had to
listen. Then he would understand. He had to!

He glanced at her hand in disgust, shaking it off.

'Next time, pretend a little more, *Amanda*. At least
tell the guy once that you love him, even though it will
be a lie, too.'

'I do. It's not a lie. Mac, listen to me.' She was close
to tears; he could not be so implacable that he
wouldn't even listen to her.

'I've heard it all before, Mandy, from Liza,' he
ground out, turned and stalked away, back rigid with
disapproval, visage black.

Amanda started to follow, but was again impeded
then blocked by more fans clamouring for autographs,
for a word from her. As her identity spread, more and
more of Timber's residents came over, some for
pictures and one or two that she knew to speak to her.
The girl who had been so friendly in the drugstore
came over. 'Fancy you being so famous. I don't think
we'll call it Cora's house much longer.'

Amanda laughed with her, though her eyes scanned
the crowds, trying to locate Mac.

Martin Stevens came up to her, reminiscing about
the day she bought Cora's house. Pam Haversham
joined them, then Elizabeth Burke and, lastly, John-
Michael. Elizabeth spoke first.

'My dear, John-Michael tells me you are quite
famous, that it is quite a feather in our cap to have you

for our festival. I'm so pleased, but I'm sorry I didn't realise it before. We are indebted to you for joining us today.'

'I'm glad to do it, Elizabeth. I still plan to make Timber my home. I want to contribute to my home town's events, too. If it is something people like, good.'

John-Michael gave her a quick hug, much to the amazement of the onlookers. 'Glad to see you, Mom,' he teased.

Amanda threw him an anguished look. 'I'm not sure it's still on. Your dad's so mad at me.'

'Mac? Nonsense. He'll be delighted to find out who you are and that the festival has such outstanding talent today. He'll like it when he sees all we have done,' Elizabeth said firmly. 'I'm so glad he came this year.'

Amanda smiled, nodding.

'John-Michael, why did you call her Mom?' Pam Haversham asked, picking up on his words.

He looked questioningly at Amanda, then grinned at Pam. 'I guess they're announcing it today. Dad's asked her to marry him.' John-Michael grinned proudly.

Elizabeth stared at them, first one, then the other, mouth agape. Finally summoning her wits she said, 'I never thought I'd see the day. Welcome to the family, child. Good gracious!' Miss Burke was bereft of words, as she gave Amanda a brief hug.

'Well, I'm surprised,' Pam added. 'Best wishes and all that!'

'Thanks, Pam, I . . .'

'Come for a last minute check, Mandy,' Dave called from the bus.

Excusing herself with a promise to join them all after the show, she moved to the bus.

'Where's the happy groom?' Dave asked, scanning

the crowds much as Amanda had just moments earlier.
His beard was trimmed for the show, his cowboy
outfit ornate with silver and embroidery.

'Flaming angry with me,' she replied, climbing into
the bus.

Briefly, while she refreshed her make-up, she
explained. While her cousin disliked the thought of
her living so far away from the action, he understood
her desire to marry the one whom she thought would
bring her as much happiness as his Evie brought him.

'I'll talk to him, if you like,' Dave offered when she
had finished.

'No, I can't use a go-between all my life. Thanks
anyway. I'll just hunt him up after the show and make
him listen to me. I have some rights in this too, you
know,' she said spiritedly.

'Show time.' Joe popped his head in.

Taking a deep breath, Amanda gave a dazzling
smile. 'I'm ready.'

The day was warm, the sun shone in a cloudless sky,
but a gentle breeze kept the air temperate. There were
people milling around, some playing the games at the
far end of the field. Many were still eating, enjoying
the festive atmosphere, enjoying the camaraderie of
their friends and neighbours in this, the last big
community event before the inclement weather forced
people to keep indoors. The majority of the town,
however, was seated on the benches and chairs set up
for the entertainment event. A large group of young
people were lounging on blankets on the grass near the
stage.

Amanda and Dave walked together to the steps at
the rear of the portable stage. The disjointed twang of
guitars being tuned, of amplifiers being adjusted,
could be heard over the noise of the crowd. Amanda
paused, feeling the surge of adrenalin that preceded
performances. She loved it. The excitement, the

challenge of bringing pleasure and entertainment to hundreds of people. All through the gift of music that had been given to her. She realised she was fortunate in her chosen field. A lot of luck went into their achieving stardom, and in such a relatively short time, less than ten years. Still, they all had worked hard to be where they were, Dave, Sam, Joe, Marc, and Phil. They were a team and she would never want to give it up, not completely.

If she married Mac; no, she lifted her chin, *when* she married Mac, she would curtail some of the travelling, but not all. She loved it too much to quit. He would have to take this part of her as well as the rest of her. This career had contributed to making her the person she was today, the one he had asked to marry him.

She heard the opening music, mounted the stairs and burst out into view to the thunderous applause of the citizens of Timber. Taking the microphone from Dave with a bright smile, she launched immediately into the first song, 'Riverboat gambler, you take too many chances . . .' The applause swelled as the audience expressed their approval, drowning out the first few lines, then died away as everyone settled back to enjoy familiar songs performed by a top professional.

Amanda did her best for her new town, her band backing her to the limit. As she sang, joyfully, with great enthusiasm, she let her eyes browse through the crowd, recognising people here and there; a committee member she had met at Elizabeth's; the old man from the bus depot; John-Michael. With a small shock she saw Mac seated beside his son, his aunt on his other side. His hat was pulled low, shading his features. Her eyes passed on. Sally Sutherland and her father were on the far side of Elizabeth; Pam and Ron Haversham back towards the rear of the crowd.

When she finished her first song she moved right

into *Heartbroken Dreamer* ... another popular song. And then another. And another.

When the series ended, the band became quiet. Amanda, smiling brightly, waited for the applause to die down, then spoke to the crowd.

'Happy Labor Day.' She smiled again as the people clapped, whistled, yelled back. It was an exuberant group. Easy to please, warm and friendly.

'Thank you for your warm welcome. We're glad to be here.'

Again she had to pause, happiness and goodwill welling up inside her at the enthusiastic reception.

'I'd like to introduce everyone up here to you. As a lot of you already know, we're a family group. Didn't plan on it, it just happened. We all grew up together in a little town outside Durango, in Colorado. Played together, ventured forth together. And, here we are. On the drums, cousin Sam Perkins, on Mama's side, you know. Bass guitar, Phil Perkins, Sam's brother. Rhythm guitar, Joe Williams, Mama's side again. Electric piano, Marc Johnson. Mama is part of a large family.'

The crowd, applauding after each introduction, roared with laughter.

'My main man, manager, promoter, dearest friend and cousin, on *Daddy's* side, Dave Smith.'

Amanda waited for silence before continuing.

'As some of you know, I moved to Timber a few months ago, bought Cora Rosefeld's old place. I figure in fifty years or so you will call it Mandy's old place, or old Mandy's place, by then ... Timber's a grand place to live ...'

The crowd would not let her continue, they showed their approval in a thunderous round.

'And ... I have written a few songs since I've been here. I want to share them with you. If they bomb out, maybe as neighbours, you'll let me down easy.'

She nodded to Dave and, when the clapping diminished, the music started.

'Bluebells on the hill, nodding in the hot Sierra sun . . .' She sang the song she'd first written, in the early days of her life in Timber, to an enthusiastic response. She followed it with the second one she had done. Moving into a duet with Dave, a slow ballad, then song after song made famous over the last five years. All were recognised, liked, popular. The programme ran far, far longer than Elizabeth's estimated hour, but no one seemed anxious for it to end.

Finally she dropped the microphone beside her legs, turning to Dave for a quick moment, then back to the audience.

'Two more and we'll call it quits.'

Groans and protests arose from the townsfolk. She raised a hand.

'One of them is the most recent one I wrote here.'

She licked her lips nervously, again looked at Dave, grinning at her.

'Remember,' she said for him alone, 'when this one is done, go right into *Sing the Mountain Down*. Don't pause at all.'

'They'll love it,' he encouraged.

She took a breath, waiting for the music's cue.

Her strong, clear alto rose over the crowd, filling every corner of the field with the sweet harmony, the words sung simply, clearly and from her heart.

'She didn't need the mike,' one listener said afterwards.

'Beautiful, strong voice, lovely song,' said another.

'Did you see his face?' asked a third. 'I watched him, you know, I saw it.'

Amanda's voice carried conviction as her voice swelled for the chorus, her eyes only for Mac now,

'. . . I love a rancher . . . I love a rancher . . .'

Mac stared back at her, too far away for Amanda to see him clearly, to see how he was taking her song. She noticed John-Michael looked at his dad, with a grin as big as his face, but Mac steadfastly regarded Amanda.

'. . . And glory be, glory be, . . . the rancher loves me . . .'

People turned to look at Mac, neighbour nudging neighbour as the word spread. Grins appeared on faces, attention split between the singer and Mac MacKensie.

'Look at his eyes.' A neighbour nudged a friend.

'The song is about Mac Mackensie.'

'The song's right, too, he looks as if he adores her,' the friend replied.

Again and again the chorus rang out, filling the fairground of Timber, California, filling the people's minds and hearts with delight.

'. . . I love a rancher . . . and glory be, the rancher loves me . . .'

The audience went wild. Stood as they clapped and whistled and cheered. On and on the thunderous ovation continued. Amanda blinked her eyes, trying to clear them of the tears that blurred her vision, smiling tremulously at the people. She turned to Dave, with a questioning look; why no lead into the next song? He just smiled and shrugged. No point, who would hear with the noise the audience was making?

Amanda turned back to the crowd. She could no longer see Mac, nor others she knew, just a sea of happy, applauding fans. She bowed again and again, happy they liked her song. How had Mac liked it? That was the real question.

As soon as the tumult died a little, Dave started up the music. *Sing the Mountain Down* had hit the top of the charts, was still very popular and soon she was well into it. Into it and finished. At last, the show was over.

Again and again she bowed her thanks for their applause, motioning to the band, to Dave. Smiling, waving. Finally, for the last time. Then she turned and walked quickly back to the rear of the stage, stumbled down the steps, right into Mac's arms.

'I said I was a fool,' he murmured, gathering her in and lowering his head.

The touch of his mouth drove all conscious thought from Amanda's head. She clasped him tightly and returned his kisses, hungry for them. Longing and desire rising. Wishing the moment could go on and on, only the two of them, together again at last. His mouth warm and exciting, his hands moulding her against him.

'Was that a proposal up there?' he asked, when he at last raised his head.

'Please, I'm an engaged lady, I don't make proposals.' She smiled up at him, love shining from her eyes, oblivious to all going on around them.

'It was quite a song. You have a beautiful way with words, sweetheart.'

'Like, I love you?'

'Umm, just like that.' He lowered his head again to her waiting lips.

'Excuse us, but you're blocking the way.' Dave stood on the bottom step, Sam and Joe close behind.

'Oh, sorry. Dave, Sam, Joe, this is Mac!' Amanda turned around, smiling in her happiness, linking her arm in his and introducing him.

'We've sort of met,' Dave said, hesitantly offering a hand.

'Yes.' Mac took it. 'But with a misconception; I thought you were her hippie lover.'

Amanda giggled. That was something else to be cleared up. She had forgotten Mac was still in the dark about a lot of things.

'Hippie!' Dave sputtered, outrage evident in his

face. Sam kindly bumped him along before he could explode.

'Glad to meet the rancher. How did you like her song?'

Joe also shook his hand, as did Phil and Marc, now joining them.

'I liked the song. I expect most of the town liked it.' he said drily. 'I wasn't expecting anything like it. I've never had a song written to me before.' He turned and glanced warmly at Amanda's upturned face. 'I liked it very much,' he repeated.

'We thought it was good, too.'

Mac turned back to the band. 'I reckon I'll be seeing a lot of you all, if I throw my lot in with this baggage,' Mac said, drawing her close to him.

'Right on,' Dave said, still annoyed at being thought a hippie. 'But from what Mandy has lined up, not until October.'

One or two other people were coming around the stage, more behind them.

'I'll look forward to it,' Mac said hastily, his eye on the group approaching. To Amanda he spoke, turning her towards the truck. 'I have a few things I want cleared up, are you finished? Can we leave?'

'Yes, let's go. See you later,' she called over her shoulder. 'Enjoy the picnic.'

In only moments, they were pulling out of the parking lot, leaving the crowds behind, just the two of them heading for the ranch.

'I'm sorry you found out the way you did,' Amanda began diffidently. 'I don't blame you a bit for being so angry. I wanted to tell you earlier in the summer, but never found the right time. Then the rest happened so fast, your proposal, John-Michael's interruption, then the news about Evie.'

'How is she, by the way,' Mac interrupted.

'Oh, she is just fine, or will be soon. Complete

recovery. She's Dave's wife, you know. I'm very fond of her.'

'No, I didn't know Dave was married. In fact, I know very little about you other than you are headstrong and stubborn and fill my days with joy,' Mac replied.

A lump caught in her throat at the unexpected compliment.

'Oh, Mac, I've missed you so much.'

'I've missed you, too. God, I thought the time would never pass. Each night seemed five years long. Then to drive in this morning and see that bus.' He drew in a ragged breath. 'John-Michael told me who you really were. He knew, but hadn't said anything.'

'Oh, Mac. I should have told you before, but with one thing and another, I just didn't. I'm sorry you found out that way this morning.'

'We didn't communicate well when you were gone. I thought you didn't come back because you didn't want to.'

'Oh, no. I had to help with Evie. I wanted to write, then thought I should tell you personally about things ... I missed you so much,' she said, placing a consoling hand on his hard thigh.

'Tell me about you,' he said, reaching out to squeeze her hand lying on his leg.

So Amanda did, all about the incognito summer, about Dave and Evie and baby Samantha.

'And so I wrote the song. I could never seem to just come out and tell you,' she finished.

He pulled into the driveway and stopped, turning to her.

'But, Mandy love, I especially want you to say whatever you like to me. For you to feel safe and secure in our life together, to be at ease always with me. I made mistakes in my first marriage. I don't plan to repeat them this go round. If I live to be a hundred-

and-three, I want you there with me, singing your songs, panning for gold, whatever it is you want.'

'I want to be with you,' she said softly. 'I love you, Mac.'

'I love you, sweetheart.' He took her in his arms, kissing her deeply as a man long deprived, his mouth warm and exciting, evoking the responses Amanda remembered all so well. Eagerly she returned his kiss, her mouth a soft inviting sweetness to him, her hands re-learning him. Slowly she trailed fingers down the strong column of his neck, slipping beneath the collar of his shirt. His skin was warm and taut.

He left her mouth to trail kisses along her neck, to her cheeks.

'What about Sally Sutherland?' she asked abruptly.

Mac drew back just a little. 'Sally? What about Sally?'

He was totally at a loss.

'Well, she was very possessive at your aunt's dinner party, and then sat near you today and all . . .' Amanda vaguely trailed off. 'I thought perhaps you had something . . .'

'I fell in love with a hot-tempered brat the day I kissed her and she doused me with icy water. I have never loved Sally, nor given her two thoughts since falling in love with you.'

'That's when?' She laughed. 'But I had no idea!'

'Well, no,' he replied rather sheepishly. 'I, er, had to break down my own reservations first. But that's why I arranged for the option. I thought I could tie up the land for the future and be able to stop trying to get you to leave. That was the last thing I wanted by that time.'

'Oh, darling, and I never knew. I thought to give you the land for a wedding present.'

'You did? Thanks, but I don't seem to have the same urgency for it now. I'd rather have you.'

'Oh, well, it will just be in the family. You were a long time in overcoming your own reservations.'

He pulled her against him again. 'Yes, but once gone, there was only you. Here I thought I was going to have to reform a hippie wife and find instead a leading star in my life.'

'You don't mind too much, do you? she asked anxiously. 'I am planning to settle down. My engagements won't be too extensive.'

'As long as you always come back to me, I can spare you to the rest of the world a few times a year, I guess.'

'I love you John MacKensie.'

'And I love you, Mandy Smith.'

His mouth was warm and exciting and she arched against him, wondering if they'd ever be close enough to satisfy her, to feel the hard length of him against her again, to find fulfilment of the promise of his touch.

Releasing her at long last, he sat back, started the truck, reversing out to the highway.

'Are we going back to the picnic?' Amanda asked in surprise.

'No, Nevada. We can get there in only a couple of hours.'

'Nevada, whatever for?' She had thought they would go to her cabin or his home. Be alone for a while, catch up on things.

'Two reasons, one, they have twenty-four-hour marriage chapels with no waiting, and two, a motel where the phone won't ring, nor kids interrupt, nor aunts drop by. Dave said you don't have commitments until October. We can get started on a honeymoon at least.'

Amanda gave a gurgle of laughter. What about her band? Elizabeth? John-Michael? No matter. Things would work out. She sat back to enjoy the ride, to enjoy whatever life brought her and Mac together.

'. . . . Glory be, glory be, the rancher loves me.'

✦ *Harlequin Romance*

Coming Next Month

2779   ONLY A WOMAN Bethany Campbell
A sports reporter's first assignment in Fayetteville, Arkansas, brings her face-to-face with a basketball coach whose game plan puts her job—and her heart—on the line.

2780   A FOOL TO SAY YES Sandra Clark
After accusing a therapist of giving his mother false hope of walking again, a wealthy English landowner tries to involve her in an affair. What kind of fool does he take her for?

2781   THE RIGHT TIME Maura McGiveny
It's painful to come across the right man when he belongs to someone else—especially for a young woman who rejected the same man six years ago when she followed bad advice.

2782   THE PLUMED SERPENT Anabel Murray
Seeing him again brings back everything—the three days they spent together in the jungles of Mexico, the danger, the love and the heartache. What does he want with her now?

2783   GAME OF HAZARD Kate Walker
An intruder at an isolated cottage on the Yorkshire moors startles a British knitwear designer until she realizes the man needs her help—and must accept her love.

2784   THE TIGER'S CAGE Margaret Way
Trapped! A young widow with her son feels cornered when her husband's cousin hunts them down. Why won't he leave her—and her memories—alone?

Available in August wherever paperback books are sold, or through Harlequin Reader Service.

In the U.S.
P.O. Box 1397
Buffalo, N.Y.
14240-1397

In Canada
P.O. Box 2800, Postal Station A
5170 Yonge Street
Willowdale, Ontario M2N 6J3

ATTRACTIVE, SPACE SAVING BOOK RACK

Display your most prized novels on this handsome and sturdy book rack. The hand-rubbed walnut finish will blend into your library decor with quiet elegance, providing a practical organizer for your favorite hard-or soft-covered books.

Only $9.95

Approximately 16" x 8" when assembled

Assembles in seconds!

To order, rush your name, address and zip code, along with a check or money order for $10.70 ($9.95 plus 75¢ postage and handling) (New York residents add appropriate sales tax), payable to *Harlequin Reader Service* to:

In the U.S.

Harlequin Reader Service
Book Rack Offer
901 Fuhrmann Blvd.
P.O. Box 1325
Buffalo, NY 14269-1325

Offer not available in Canada.

BKR–1

Take 4 books & a surprise gift FREE

SPECIAL LIMITED-TIME OFFER

Mail to   **Harlequin Reader Service**®

In the U.S.	In Canada
901 Fuhrmann Blvd.	P.O. Box 2800, Station "A"
P.O. Box 1394	5170 Yonge Street
Buffalo, N.Y. 14240-1394	Willowdale, Ontario M2N 6J3

YES! Please send me 4 free Harlequin Romance® novels and my free surprise gift. Then send me 6 brand-new novels every month as they come off the presses. Bill me at the low price of $1.65 each ($1.75 in Canada)—a 11% saving off the retail price. There are no shipping, handling or other hidden costs. There is no minimum number of books I must purchase. I can always return a shipment and cancel at any time. Even if I never buy another book from Harlequin, the 4 free novels and the surprise gift are mine to keep forever.

116-BPR-BP6F

Name _____ (PLEASE PRINT)

Address _____ Apt. No.

City _____ State/Prov. _____ Zip/Postal Code

This offer is limited to one order per household and not valid to present subscribers. Price is subject to change.

DOR-SUB-1R

*Shay Flanagan is Gypsy,
the raven-haired beauty who inflamed passion
in the hearts of two Falconer men.*

Carole Mortimer

GYPSY

Lyon Falconer, a law unto himself, claimed Shay—when he didn't have the right. Ricky Falconer, gentle and loving married Shay—when she had no other choice.

Now her husband's death brings Shay back within Lyon's grasp. Once and for all Lyon intends to prove that Shay has always been—will always be—*his* Gypsy!

GYP–A–1